Advance Praise for *H[air for Men]*

"A blast of genius … incredibly funny and dirty in the best way, and it is frigging moving."

—Michael Redhill, author of *Bellevue Square*

"I love everything Michelle Winters writes. Nobody understands music, or masculinity, or the mosh pit battle of the sexes better. *Hair for Men* is furious, funny, and wise. Singing and screaming at the same time, it cuts to the hardest, most tender, core of our abusive, apologizing world."

—Alexander MacLeod, author of *Animal Person*

"A little book that feels like a major event. Smart, funny, and unapologetically feminist, *Hair for Men* explores the costs of patriarchy with unexpected panache. I didn't want it to end."

—Sara Levine, author of *Treasure Island!!!*

"Every so often you read a book that makes you jealous—of the writer's skill, yes, but also of future readers who haven't yet discovered its wonders. This is one of those books. Irreverent, beautifully written, heartfelt, and humane, Michelle Winters's *Hair for Men* is just as curious and charming as the title suggests. A true gift."

—Andrew David MacDonald, author of *When We Were Vikings*

"Michelle Winters is one of the most exciting writers in Canada today, and I am her biggest fan."

—Alison Pick, author of *Strangers with the Same Dream*

HAIR FOR MEN

HAIR FOR MEN*

*A NOVEL

MICHELLE WINTERS

ANANSI

Published in Canada in 2024 and the USA in 2024 by House of Anansi Press Inc.
houseofanansi.com

28 27 26 25 24   1 2 3 4 5

Library and Archives Canada Cataloguing in Publication

Title: Hair for men : a novel / Michelle Winters.
Names: Winters, Michelle, 1972- author.
Identifiers: Canadiana (print) 20230621961 | Canadiana (ebook) 2023062197X | ISBN 9781487011918 (softcover) | ISBN 9781487011925 (EPUB)
Subjects: LCGFT: Novels.
Classification: LCC PS8645.I5762 H35 2024 | DDC C813/.6—dc23

Cover design: Greg Tabor
Cover image: Barber's chair by Rakhimov Edgar @ Shutterstock
Book design and typesetting: Lucia Kim

House of Anansi Press is grateful for the privilege to work on and create from the Traditional Territory of many Nations, including the Anishinabeg, the Wendat, and the Haudenosaunee, as well as the Treaty Lands of the Mississaugas of the Credit.

With the participation of the Government of Canada
Avec la participation du gouvernement du Canada | Canadä

We acknowledge for their financial support of our publishing program the Canada Council for the Arts, the Ontario Arts Council, and the Government of Canada.

Printed and bound in Canada

for Peter Winters

My optimism wears heavy boots and is loud.
—*Henry Rollins*

2016

AT THE EDGE OF THE PIER, I crouch and slide the duffle bag from my shoulder into the little yellow boat, careful not to smear any blood on the decking. The bag is heavier than usual, and I force air through my nose to slow my breath. Behind me, the marina is asleep. I look back and count the six lights that stay on all night: the three in the parking lot, the beacon on the clubhouse peak, and the two hard-wired emergency units flanking the sign out front that says Cradle Bay Boat Club. Everything else is dark, most importantly, the Commodore's office on the ground floor.

I climb down into the Eraserhead, and the boat dips, bringing the gunwales a few inches closer to the surface. Aside from me and the bag, not much else fits in the cockpit of the thirteen-footer. I take another look back at the yard as I unfasten the line from the cleat and push off.

My bow cuts the moonlit ripples and I raise the mainsail, securing it and holding the edge of the boom as it catches the breeze. I raise and trim the jib and sail silently out, tacking around the end of the cove into The Mistake. When you're leaving the marina for the Bay of Fundy, you instinctively approach the harbour through a channel on your starboard side, but after about two kilometres you start seeing land close in around you and realize it's not a channel, it's an inlet. You have to go the whole way back and start again on the other side of the spit. It wastes about an hour and a half under power. Only visiting vessels get stuck in there, and only if we don't warn them. The enclosure of the inlet, furthermore, kills the wind just enough to make it a haven for horseflies, so there's no reason for anyone to go in there. Just the place to dump the bodies.

Inside the cove, I release the sails so they billow gently. I unzip the bag.

My hand touches something cold and hairy. It's a man's leg, soft and white with dark hair, foot laced into a Nike Air Max Plus. I don't recognize the shoe, but I never really looked at shoes. Scalps, sure. Necks, ears ... If you spend enough time looking at scalps and ears, you can make them disappear. Over time, my eyes learned to skim right past the eczema and acne without ever touching down. It's a skill I use at the marina's intake dock when I'm cleaning out a holding tank, and I consider it one of my greater feats of self-restraint. The Nike could belong to Huey; he used to play pickup with his brother. Or Wei? He was on a softball team ... They usually arrived in work clothes, since it was daytime. A ton of them played sports—some of them in earnest, some of them to try to develop relationships with other men. I stuff the leg in a garbage bag, then add a rock, and hold the whole package against my chest to force out the air before twisting and knotting the top. I slip the bag into the water, and it sinks with a burp.

Reaching back into the duffle, I pull out a forearm, more tanned than the leg, wrist encircled by an oversized TAG Heuer watch with a steel band. The arm's black hairs are caught between the links. The arm is turning green, and death has puffed it up, but you can still see the structure and tone of a middle-aged man. The hand is beautiful, the fingers long and curved with powerful knuckles. I stuff it in a new plastic bag.

A horsefly buzzes past my ear and I swat it dead on the deck, shooting a little echo around the cove. I take out a sport-socked foot and sink it. Then another hand, just past the wrist, and an upper arm with a bulky bicep. No head. I zip up the remaining rocks in the duffle and release it over the side, watching the bubbles rise to the surface and disappear.

I take the bailer (a bleach bottle with the bottom cut out), fill it with water, and swish it around the cockpit. The blood swirls down the drainage hole. I fill bailer after bailer until the cockpit glistens white in the moonlight. When I'm done, I reach into the water to wash my hands. Something clamps onto my wrist. It's the hand wearing the TAG Heuer watch.

I try to pull free, but the cold hand grips my thumb and tries to pry open my fingers. I get down low in the cockpit and thrash my arm, but then a third hand grabs me and tries to stuff a hundred-dollar bill into my fist. I pull and pull until my arm snaps back against the ceiling above my cast-off sleeping bag. I shoot upright in the forward berth of The Pill and a droplet of morning condensation drips from the hatch onto my forehead. I fall back into the pillows.

This dream has become like part of my waking life. The membrane of consciousness between the world where I dispose of bodies and the world where I don't is so thin that when I look out toward The Mistake, I can't be entirely sure it's not filled with corpses.

From one dream to the next, I can remember the location of every bag I've dropped, and I can manoeuvre the Eraserhead in my sleep to a spot uncluttered by previous dreams.

There are only ever men in the bags, which makes sense when I consider how much of my life I've devoted to them. Just when I think I've jettisoned my last bag, I find myself with another.

1988–1994

MY CAREER IN MEN'S HAIRSTYLING was preordained. My dad sold shampoo for Christof Gallant, and some of my favourite childhood summer days were spent in the car with him, driving from salon to salon around small-town Ontario in our Chevrolet Caprice, while my mother was at home in our tiny Mimico brick bungalow, drinking white wine with Mrs. Murphy from down the street. Dad introduced me to a world where women were in charge, and where his job was to please and impress them. One of the ways he did this was with free samples; the other was his masculinity. He had the cherub's head of strawberry ringlets he'd passed down to me, and he maintained it at a length that gave him a Percy Shelley virility without ever coming across as feminine. The salon ladies would get right in there and twirl fistfuls of it around their manicured fingers. Their licence to him had no restriction. It was the 1980s, and restriction was no one's thing, but when my dad gave those women a bag of conditioner samples, they literally swarmed him with kisses. They'd push him down in the shampoo chair and jump in his lap—sometimes a few of them in a stack. Their innuendo-filled exchanges taught me the art of the wink and made me feel included, even though I struggled to understand what was really going on. My dad, it goes without saying, was a champion winker.

Watching women interact with my father was as captivating to my child's mind as a kaleidoscope or *The Jungle Book*. The ladies would sit me under the bonnet dryer with a magazine, the hot noise crashing and swirling around my head like an ocean, wrapping me in velvet calm while I watched through slitted eyes to discern what it was about my dad they found so exciting. There was the physical reality of him, every flirty exchange punctuated by a touch of his chest or shoulder. Aside from the physical contact, he was charming, and he gave them the full benefit of his attention: he asked about their kids, he laughed at their jokes, he shattered their doldrums. My dad was a treat.

One time he caught my eye over a suntanned shoulder. "Lou," he said afterward, wiping lipstick off his cheek as we crossed the Timbermill Shops and More parking lot, "these ladies buy your dinner. Whatever I do with them, it's all in the interests of selling shampoo. Your mother has a hard time with that sometimes, but it's part of the job. In fact, it is the job."

"I know," I said. "They like you." Whatever misgivings

he may have had, all I saw was a healthy business model. Those women bought copiously from the Christof Gallant Shine and Balance line, and in return they enjoyed this sexy, enhanced version of my dad that he seemed glad to offer.

"They do," he said. "Those women like men."

"I like men," I said.

He stopped. "Louise, that's ... not something you can just say."

An ancient Burt Reynolds movie I wasn't allowed to watch on TV, *The Man Who Loved Women*, popped into my head.

"If Burt Reynolds can love women, why can't I love men?"

He sighed ruefully. "Well ... that won't be as easy as you think. I mean, maybe some of us ... Not now. Well, me excepted ... but then I'm not a man, I'm your father ..." He studied me sadly for a moment. "Ah, you'll figure it out." Then he bopped me on the head. "Race you to the car!" He took off at top speed, knees high, and smacked the hood on arrival. "I win again!"

✂

My dad was toughening me up, I realized later, for a world orchestrated to my disadvantage. The stirrings were every-where. I remember the night Tony Wickett from a few doors down came over to announce the birth of his son. Tony was smoking a cigar, handed one to my dad, slapped him on the arm, and said, "My friend, it's a boy. Jee*zus*, what a relief!" And they laughed. When I came around the doorway to ask why boys were a relief, Tony Wickett crouched down to assure me, with Grinchy finesse, "Oh, honey, we'd have been just as happy with a girl."

Minor disagreements my dad would propose we settle by arm wrestling, me at 65 pounds, he at 190. He'd clear a space at the dinner table, sit with an elbow propped on the edge, fingers fanned. We'd face off. As I'd gnash my teeth, straining to leverage his wrist, he'd casually croon, "Let me know when you're ready to start." The shit-talking was as central as his guaranteed victory. Every night when he tucked me in, he'd beat me at cribbage, so that my final awareness before drifting off was just how hard I had to try against someone who didn't seem to try at all. At the same time, my dad campaigned for my subjugation of Barry Murphy, son of Mrs. Murphy from down the street. When Mrs. Murphy would come over to drink white wine and complain about men with my mom ("Gene's got a Christ complex, that's his problem"), Barry and I would play in the basement, and my dad would debrief me afterward.

"So what did you and Barry get up to?"

"Played G.I. Joes. Climbed the tree."

"Kick his ass?"

"I guess?"

"Good girl!"

From the stove, my mom would lean on a post—Mrs. Murphy

hip and say, "Oh, good job, Paul. Now you've got her full attention, make sure you steer her right."

Mom was my first favourite: warm, smelled good, picked me up ... but the more I felt the real-life disfavour of girlhood—and her antipathy toward men—the more distance I put between us, devoting myself entirely to my dad. Mom and I cultivated an inert rivalry based on the sad, unspoken truth that we'd started out as allies.

The quandary for my young brain was how the salon ladies managed to resist falling victim to the feminine condition Barry's mom came over to rail against. I could only conclude it had to do with their love of men. I knew early on I'd be one of them. I started cutting my own hair at home with my mother's sewing scissors, having carefully observed all my own haircuts, and knew my technique was solid. But I couldn't quite picture myself among their coral-coloured ranks—the touching, the flirting. How did one pick that up?

✄

The summer I turned sixteen, femininity reared up and staked its indelible claim. I shot up to six feet, and my breasts ballooned. I'd always flown unremarkably beneath the bullying radar; now I was conspicuous all the time. I lashed myself down with sports bras and tank tops and learned to walk with my back hunched like a turtle, trying to look shorter and flatter. Already losing ground in the world of boys—Barry wouldn't talk to me at school anymore because we were "on different teams now" and he said I should find other girls to hang out with—much of my psyche became preoccupied with hiding my body. My clothes felt invisible, my nakedness exhausting. I'd taken down the mirror from the back of my bedroom door.

Starting high school meant taking a city bus, which meant a whole new bus stop where I waited in the mornings with two older boys from school, Mitch and Spence. They were in Grade 13 when I was in Grade 10, so we didn't run in the same circles, but I knew them in the way you get to know older kids. Spence was big and dumb and played rugby, while Mitch was littler and meaner; he wore a bomber-type jacket like he was from the 1950s. His hair was crunchy with gel, the way boys wore it in the 1980s. Like plastic. His nose was like a little button beneath two shiny black eyes deep-set into cold sockets. He was frustratingly handsome. In my nascent appreciation of men, he was a clear-skinned, black-haired, wealthy, freckled specimen of perfection, light years from my plain, tomboyish world. He had a leering snicker and nodded his head constantly in smug accord. He and Spence were a strange combination, coming from different social groups—they didn't look like they even lived in the same decade—but they never ran out of things to talk about. Spence laughed at Mitch's every word, the nastier the better, and Mitch clearly chose words he knew Spence would like. When I'd get to the bus stop in the morning, they'd be there, talking about the two things that cemented their friendship: The Tragically Hip and pussy.

"Thompson says he can't come see the Hip with us Saturday. He has to have dinner at Shelly's."

"You don't see me sticking around for dinner at Lisa's. I just wipe off my dick and get out."

"Hyuk, hyuk, I wipe mine on Stephanie's mom's drapes!"

I tried not to show I was listening, but my face would flame, my knees would tremble, and even though I kept my hunched back to them, it never took long before they noticed me.

"You think anyone's fucking her?"

"You crazy? Look at her! She should be on the fuckin' team."

"Right on. Tits are massive, though."

"You'd have to reach over your head to get a handful."

"Can you shut up?" I somehow found the courage to speak. They paused for a second, then laughed.

"Think she's ever been titfucked?"

I could have walked to the next stop, I could have gone another eight minutes out of my way to escape them—I could even have walked the whole way to school in about forty minutes—but I didn't, because it was my goddamned stop too. Besides, I was perversely flattered by the attention. I crossed my arms and watched, rabbit-hearted, for the bus to appear down the street, pretending I didn't care.

"Even if she was on her knees, you'd have to stand on a chair to get your dick in her mouth."

After a while of this, they'd start to scream-sing parts of

Tragically Hip songs, like the "*Let me ouuuuuuuuuuuut!*" part from "Locked in the Trunk of a Car," or "*At the Hundredth Meridian! (At the Hundredth Meridian!) At the Hundredth Meridian! (At the Hundredth Meridian!)*." It signalled the moment they'd lost interest in me—then they'd go back to talking like I wasn't there.

Once we'd boarded the bus, they forgot about me altogether. They didn't harass me at school either, probably because acknowledging me in front of other people was beneath them. The only time I crossed paths with Mitch was on my way out of Physics.

One day as our classes were squeezing past each other in the doorway, he reached out his hand and passed something to me smoothly, palm to palm. When I gaped back at him from the folded sheet of looseleaf, he smiled—a friendly smile—his face softening, erasing every disgusting word, every putrid comment, radiating just pure, sweet, masculine beauty. Out in the hall, my head buzzing, the paper dampened in my palm as I stole into the fountain alcove to open it.

I think you're so pretty. Meet me after school in the woods behind the bleachers.

The woods behind the bleachers was a legendary make-out spot for the older kids.

My heart shot out of my chest.

He was in Grade 13. *Grade 13*. With a girlfriend. Maybe he was thinking of breaking up with her. Who knows ... I'd seen Lisa around with her gaggle of pretty friends, and I'd never once registered on her radar. But he saw me. Sure, he'd said all those horrible things, but I'd watched enough TV to know that people are supposed to torture each other when they're in love. Boys are conditioned not to show their feelings. He had to act that way because Spence was around, but he'd be different in private. Well, I'd let him know his private feelings were okay with me. I folded up the note and floated to my next class, where I opened it secretly under my desk, reading it over and over. *Pretty.* I sat up tall in my chair and pulled back my shoulders, my vertebrae popping one after the other all the way down to my tailbone.

The rest of the day was a blur of fantasies: us kissing between classes, holding hands, snickering together at someone weaker ... I tried to imagine the benefits of dating someone so snarky. I figured I'd better start catching up on The Tragically Hip. I'd never really paid them much attention, even though every third song on the radio was one of theirs.

Sixth period that day was Chemistry. Mitch and Lisa would be graduating this year. Would he take me to prom? Would I have to fight Lisa? I sensed Mitch would probably find prom stupid, since he seemed to find a lot of things stupid—or maybe he was just putting that on for Spence too. I was so distracted during that final class that I grabbed the neck of the Bunsen burner and seared my hand. Mrs. Robbins told me to go to the nurse, and I said I would, but I just went to the Girls' and ran cold tap water on my fingers until the buzzer went.

From the school's back door across the field to the bleachers, I held my wet palm up to the air. I should have wrapped it, but I wasn't wasting time. Maybe Mitch would find it romantic that I'd burned myself so badly and had still gone to see him. I wished I'd been wearing something nicer. I suddenly worried that my sweatshirt and jeans were too plain, my seafoam-green Patagonia jacket too sporty, or preppy. I should start dressing cooler. Learn more about music. My stomach was everywhere. I was terrified and never happier.

Behind the bleachers, I parted the twigs and made my way down the root-tangled incline into the woods behind the school. There was a partially demolished shack where the older kids would go to drink and have sex, so I figured that's where I was headed.

"Hello?" I said, hoping to sound flirty and carefree, the way the salon ladies addressed my dad.

There was a rustling from behind the shack, and he stepped out, hands in the pockets of his bomber.

"Hey, you," he said in a cold purr I'd never heard him use around Spence, one I'd certainly never heard my dad use with the ladies.

We smiled at each other, and I wondered if I should run to him, but that felt dramatic, so I just walked very, very quickly. He took a step back.

"Whoa." He held up his hands.

Play it cool.

"You got here early," I said. Conversational? Flirty?

"Yeah ... I cut English."

"Cool." I laughed. "Look, I burned my hand in Chemistry."

"Uh, wow," he said, "that looks bad."

I laughed again (desperately?). "It's okay, it doesn't hurt that much."

"Oh-kay ..."

I could feel I wasn't doing what he wanted. *Stop talking. Let him lead.*

"Here, c'mon back here," he said, gesturing behind the shack. I followed him into the three-walled structure, strewn with what I panicked to instinctively identify as used condoms. I hid my hand and shrugged meekly as he came closer. *Soft and quiet.* I tried not to appear hungry as my eyes sped over his freckles, the squareness of the tip of his nose, the new stubble on his jaw—he was like a *man*. I looked at my sneakers.

So ..." he said, gazing up at me heartthrob-style from under his eyebrows. "I meant what I said."

My insides jumped. This was it. I slumped my shoulders deeper and bent my knees just slightly, trying to look tinier. Weaker.

"Yeah." He reached up and touched my hair, the ends I'd trimmed myself entwined in his fingers. "And I like that you're not a show-off about your body, even though it's ... you know, smokin'."

I kept my shoulders up, since he liked my modesty, but

sneaked my eyes up to the tendons in his neck. I secretly inhaled the Coca-Cola smell of his deodorant, deploying my olfactories to consume every nuance, my nose warming in the nearness of his chest. Delicious.

"Here," he said, reaching for the zipper of my jacket, "you don't have to hide from me."

Already feeling dangerously exposed, I panicked a little and held my breath, braced for whatever was coming. I squared my eyes on his T-shirt to calm down, on the word *Tragic* revealed by the edges of his bomber. He lifted the bottom of my sweatshirt and whispered, "So pretty." I sucked in my belly, urging myself through the portal to the next phase of my maturity. His would be the first eyes on me apart from my parents' and Dr. Gilani's—the shift felt like the first moments on a roller coaster, when the car gets jostled onto the belt and your only choice is to go along.

I lifted my arms as he fought his way under my tank top and bra, hoisting them up to my armpits, the fall air hitting my skin. "Here, turn this way …" he said. I stared and stared at his T-shirt, eyes wide and welling with tears. I couldn't understand why. His hands came up gently under my breasts and cupped them, then he moved around the sides and squeezed them together—strangely, it felt a little like being at the doctor, but I vowed not to be a baby. Only when he put a hand underneath each one and started to smack them up and down did the reflex finally kick in to stop him—right at the moment a splutter of laughter burst over his shoulder.

I looked up to see Spence peering around the partial wall at the far end, covering his red face with both hands as he exploded in gales of laughter. He disappeared, and I heard him just scream—*scream*—with joy. His laughter made Mitch's face crumple, and I turned my back to them both, grabbing for the band of my bra with my burned hand, wrestling for cover. I windmilled my arms to close my jacket and grabbed my backpack from the ground. My fists flexed, and I stood there searching for something, *anything*, to say, which only made them laugh harder. Hot tears of rage threatened to erupt for real, so I jammed my arms into the straps of my backpack and took off, but my backpack wouldn't budge, and when I peeked over my shoulder, Spence was holding onto it, looking eagerly to Mitch for some kind of cue. I thrashed in his grip, unwilling to yield my belongings, until Mitch said, "Aw, let her go," and I went flying past them into the trees with the momentum. I had scrambled up the incline and was halfway across the football field, their laughter still ringing, when I heard them start a round of "*Let me ouuuuuuuuuuuut!!!*" which was almost worse than the laughter, because it meant they'd moved on, like they always did. They weren't yelling about me or my escape; it was just a song.

My sneakers smacked the ground double time across the football field, the parking lot, and down Kipling. My tears evaporated in the onrush of air, my epiglottis perched on the edge of a scream. I didn't need to look back to know they weren't following, but I couldn't stop moving, knowing the moment I did, reality would land. As I raced onto Lakeshore I balled a fist and, with no one else to hit, knocked it against my temple. Idiot. Duck. Lamb. Fuck. I ran past the Ultramar, Coffee Time, the strip mall with the dry cleaner, dentist, and nail salon, my sneakers slapping the concrete—*plack*, *plack*, *plack*—until I heard a scream.

I skidded to a stop.

A man's raw-throated, furious bellow blasted from the open door of a smoky little shop called Haller's Records. I gasped—my first real breath in blocks—my lungs inflating to capacity as I found myself swaying to the loudest, fastest, angriest noise I'd ever heard. Everything else narrowed to a point, concentrated in the eye of what pulsed from that store's speakers. My head felt cushioned in suspended animation, as though everything else around me had stopped mid-movement while the only force at work in the universe raged here. The song ended, and another one, indistinguishable from the first, started playing. I couldn't move. The speed and aggression soothed me like—what? It took a second for the body memory to hit: like a salon's bonnet dryer.

Through the doorway, past a raft of skateboards, a group of lanky guys, some with long hair, some with buzz cuts, one with shaved sides and the top long, flanked the counter. They were nodding. A couple of them wore leather jackets with skeleton faces painted in Liquid Paper on the back; a few wore army gear. I recognized one guy with long, frizzly brown hair.

I'd seen him smoking and doing skateboard tricks in Amos Waite Park. He might have been a grown-up.

I stood in the doorway, blocking the entrance, paralyzed. I half considered bolting, but the music ... Finally, an albino-white-haired guy at the counter looked up and lifted his chin. I picked my way to the counter, and he raised his invisible eyebrows. Outside my control, my arm floated up and my index finger pointed to the sky. "What's this?" He lifted his chin again and I summoned all my air to release the voice I hadn't been able to find back in the woods.

"WHAT'S!!! THIS!!!"

He gave me a quick once-over, then picked up a CD case and held it out. The cover showed a black-and-white photo of a guy with a shaved head punching his own reflection in a shattered mirror. Big red letters spelled out BLACK FLAG, DAMAGED.

"CAN I BUY IT?"

The guys nodded and the one behind the counter picked up a fresh copy from the rack.

"IT'S A HARDCORE CLASSIC." He rang it up and handed me my change. "THIS IS ROLLINS'S FIRST ALBUM WITH THEM."

I nodded back, holding the magical square in my seared palm like a compass.

>✁

At home, my mother and Mrs. Murphy were shrieking with laughter in our kitchen. Boy, everything was funny that day.

"I hope he gets the sores under control before he and his secretary hit the beach at Cabo!" Mrs. Murphy screamed before the two of them melted into another high-pitched frenzy.

"Hey, sweetie." My mom's voice wafted up the stairs after me. I ran cold water over the blisters forming on my hand and wrapped it with a pillowcase.

In my room, I opened my yellow Sony Discman and pulled out Ace of Base. I scratched at my new CD's tight cellophane wrapping until I had to get a pen. The plastic *skreeked* as the case's hinge flexed open, and I brought my nose down to detect hints of ink and dry macaroni. There were no liner notes, no lyrics, just the song titles and credits written in red and the image of the man punching the mirror. I pulled out the pristine disc and set it in the player, put on my headphones, and pressed Play. As the seconds whirred by, I devoured that image, the man's bleeding fist, the glass shards splayed out from the point of impact like jagged petals. An insistent cymbal beat four times, and I cranked the tiny dial. A squeal of feedback cut in like a scratch on a record; a speeding guitar played a descending scale, countered by an ascending one, almost too fast for each other, facing off, back and forth. And then—then came the shouting: Henry Rollins's no-melody, no-singing, no-bullshit rage. The whole mess together sounded like one long screech of feedback, an offence imposed on the orderly world in exchange for the one imposed on mine, and as the music's anguish flooded through my headphones, it revealed the solution. Like bacteria to its ecosystem, I would adapt. I would trade my girl dermis for a spiky carapace you'd know better than to touch—or stare at. No more lamb. I closed my eyes and imagined poking the tip of one scissor blade into Mitch's urethra and snipping the whole way down his penis so it opened out flat like a hide.

.   When the album finished, I rose from my bed and made my way to the hall closet where Mom kept the donation bag of old clothes for the Diabetes Association. I pulled out a plaid shirt of my dad's and stuffed my sweatshirt in the bag. Locked in the upstairs bathroom with Mom's sewing shears in my unburned hand, I scowled at my reflection in the medicine cabinet mirror and imagined the thrill of punching it. Instead, I grabbed a handful of curls over my right ear and snipped, the first hunk landing in the sink like a small strawberry animal. I snipped tuft after tuft, then grabbed my dad's razor and shaved the side clean down to the skin; I nicked a spot and stopped to watch the blood escape the fresh pink wound. When the top of my hair flopped over and touched my naked scalp, I gasped, shaking the cool locks on my newly exposed flesh. Using one of the record store guys as my model, I moved to the other side, giggling uncontrollably as more and more hair fell away, revealing my naked scalp. I kept shaving, connecting the sides to the back in a kind of tophawk.

When I came downstairs for dinner, Mom screamed like she was in a horror movie. "*NO*, Louise, what did you *do???*"

I shrugged and crushed a potato on my plate.

"Well, that shirt has never looked so good! Maybe I should give you all my hand-me-downs." Classic Dad.

He treated my burned hand with Neosporin and, despite my mother's frustrated objections, drove me to TNT army surplus after dinner to buy me a whole new wardrobe. I picked out a hoodie, fatigues, and a camouflage jacket, just like the guys at the record store. Dad seemed pleased with my choices, in a beating-Barry kind of way.

"Hey, Lou, what about these pants? They're not army, but they're navy, and isn't that even more punk?" As a kid, he used to visit his grandparents in Yarmouth, Nova Scotia, and they'd go fishing off Sweeney's Wharf, where he said you could throw your unbaited hook in the water and pull up a fish in under a minute. He'd always wanted to live on the ocean. But sometimes you end up selling shampoo in Southern Ontario, and the lake is not the ocean.

"I'm hardcore, Dad."

"I'll bet none of the other hardcores at school have a pair of these!"

He was right, and they were a lot more flattering than the camouflage pants. For someone my height, the swish of flares worked. That was my first pair of bib-fronts, and they became my special occasion pants.

Rifling through a rack of coats, he pulled out a big blue one with wide lapels. "Ooh, look at this. Do you know what this is?" he said, pulling it off the hanger and holding it up.

"It's a greatcoat. Like Admiral Horatio Nelson wore. Can you try it? Come on."

I don't know how my dad's fashion sense was so spot-on. It's like he'd always wanted to be a girl who dressed like a sailor. The coat also completely hid my chest, which made it a winner.

Next, I asked for sneakers and a skateboard, insisting I needed them that very night. Dad obliged, since we were already out, and I got some regular black Vans, nothing fancy, and a Vision Gator deck. It was brand new and would need stickers and an anarchy symbol, but it would get me to school—I was done with the bus.

"Do you want me to show you how to ride that?" my dad asked at the cash.

"You can skate?"

"Growing up, this was a normal thing for boys to do."

"All right."

"Now, you're going to fall down. A lot. We should get you knee and elbow pads. And a helmet."

"I don't want them."

"I didn't think so."

It was late when we got home, but at my urging, my dad stayed out to teach me. He started me off with the basics on our short, level driveway: stepping on and walking, one foot on, one beside.

"Practise until you can do this in your sleep," he said, "until the board becomes part of you. Watch." He skated effortlessly up to the end of the driveway, doing a half-flip there that he didn't quite land. We determined my dominant foot (regular), then covered stepping on with both and stopping with the flat sole of my foot. It should have been fun to learn with my dad, but the shame that had scorched me, the whole reason I was accepting his instruction, was hardening into the beginnings of the wedge I'd drive between us so he'd never find out that I'd let myself get had.

"Well, that's enough for tonight. See you for our game?"

"Naw, I'm going to stay out here and practise," I mumbled, rolling the board back and forth.

He turned to go inside and stopped. "Is there anything you'd like to talk about, Lou?"

"No. Why?"

"It's some pretty sudden changes is all. I just wonder if you might want to tell me the reason."

I shrugged, feeling so little agency right then that withholding an explanation from my dad felt like a win.

"All right," he said. "Let me know if you change your mind."

"Whatever." I pushed off and rolled away from him, resolved not to soften. I couldn't help thinking how much he would have enjoyed the story if it had ended with me laying Spence and Mitch out cold. The thought of disappointing him made me wretched.

When I finally lay down in bed, buffeted by a continuous sense of rolling, I stared at the ceiling, my frantic mind replaying every moment in the woods. I knocked the knuckles of my good hand against my head as a reset and reviewed my foot placement, weight distribution, but my weight brought me back to my body, which brought me back to the cold afternoon air and struggling with my clothes. And the laughter. The endless laughter. And the scream-singing. Then left foot on and push with right, left foot on and push with right, until dawn, when I fell asleep for forty minutes.

When I got up, I re-bandaged my hand, put on my new gear, and got ready for school like I normally would—only instead of turning right for the bus stop, I took a left at the end of our street and headed for Amos Waite Park.

><

My chest was still burning from the day before, all the more when I considered that Mitch and Spence certainly weren't spending the day hiding out in a park. At that moment, quitting school felt like my only choice—were it not that I needed a diploma to get into Hair Academy.

The park was populated at that hour by a few moms and nannies slumped wearily as their charges enjoyed an early romp on the jungle gym. I rolled slowly past, a lifetime from child or mom, just an ugly new spawn, taking the air.

I pushed off and rode around the parking lot until I felt ready for the slight decline of the splash pad—where I immediately wiped out like a starfish. I lay on my face as my board hit a parking block on the embankment before rolling back

down into my forehead. The part of me my dad had trained
for this embraced the gallows. I'd torn a pair of my new pants
and skinned my elbow and forearm, raising tiny blood spots
from the raw underlayer of my skin. My first road rash.

As I searched for the will to get up, a car stopped at the
nearby intersection. It took a second before I heard it amid the
rest of the noise: "*Let me out!!!*" blasted from the car's open
window. All at once my whole body seized. My breathing got
shallow, and I felt suddenly topless, as if my clothes had evaporated; I heard the sound of laughter coming from all sides.
I squeezed my arms over my ears, shielding my battered head,
until the light changed and the car pulled away. So, among
my keepsakes, I'd come away with this too. It was virtually
impossible to manage everyday life in Toronto in the 1990s
without hearing The Tragically Hip.

I glanced at my watch. Second period would be just getting
out. Was there gossip by now? Had Mitch and Spence told
everyone? Were they regaling the school with tales of my
hideous body? *Louise? But she was always so shy ...*

Ha.

Of course not.

No matter how hilarious they may have found my humil-
iation, I gained them nothing in status. I knew it was a secret
best kept between them. Something they'd done together,
just a couple of friends. The banks of my anger sloshed as I
picked grit from my arm.

✂

I didn't go to school the rest of that week; I spent every day at the park. I met a few other skateboarders, including the frizzly-haired guy from the record store, whose name was Marko. He gave me some tips and showed me how to ollie, but I smashed my tailbone on my first try. Instead, I vowed to master rolling a straight line.

Friday afternoon, my mom caught me in the kitchen.

"Louise, the school called," she said, her face so distraught that I had to barricade myself behind the fridge door as I foraged.

"So?"

"Can you tell me what's wrong?"

"Makes you think something's wrong?" I said, stuffing slices of salami in my mouth. What I really wanted was to kneel before her, bawl in her lap, and tell her everything. If anyone understood masculine wrongs, it was my mom. Instead, I closed the fridge and scowled down at her, my enormous new body and terrifying hair looming over her until she stepped out of my way. This was the battle I picked. Because I felt I could win.

I pulled it together and headed to school on Monday, giving myself enough time to negotiate a skate route along the sidewalk—there was no way I was getting back on the bus—carrying my board when needed and cutting through parking lots and parkettes when possible. It took the same amount of time as the bus, but with the added fulfillment of inconvenience and the occasional spill.

My new style turned some heads, particularly among the pretty girls, who looked at me like I'd just crawled out of a sewer. But it was a relief not having to worry about ever being one of them. Attractiveness to boys was a low-level tax I'd never pay, and I enjoyed my fresh power to shock and repel. It took the pressure off.

Inevitably, I couldn't stop my heart from hammering as I scanned the halls, and my pulse ramped up as the minutes of Physics class ticked down. Then, right on cue, the buzzer rang, our class poured out, Mitch's class mashed in, and in the doorway, I met his eyes. What I'd honestly hoped as I lay in bed the night before, thoughts racing, was that he'd see me, do a double take, then be hit with remorse as he realized what he'd done— he'd also be a little apprehensive, because I must be a real loose cannon to make a change this radical. He'd pull me aside and apologize sincerely out in the hallway, where maybe he'd tell me he and Spence weren't friends anymore because he didn't want to keep having to do awful things to make Spence happy. What in fact happened was that he saw me—no double take— and gave a dismissive upward nod. "Nice hair," he snickered.

I gave myself a quick sock in the temple in the safety of a bathroom stall, hyperventilating until I hiccuped. I closed my eyes and calmed down by imagining his sinuses caving under my sneaker. I skipped my last two periods and skated down to Haller's, not sure what to do with my rage. Rolling along a clean stretch of asphalt during school hours, breaking rules—the air was rarefied. If nothing else, the licence to reject the normal world felt good.

The white-haired guy named Flemm was working. He pointed to a hand-Sharpied sign for a Bunchoffuckinggoofs show at Sneaky Dee's that night and asked if I was going.

"Are they hard?"

"They're sick. They used to have their own fort and everything, before the city ran them out." He put on a CD called *Carnival of Chaos + Carnage*. I bought a copy. When Flemm handed me my change, he looked at the brown scab on the heel of my hand and, genuinely impressed, said, "Sweet rash."

With no clue what to expect, I headed downtown, trying not to feel too weird about walking into a show alone. The pitch-black upstairs bar took care of that. I found an unoccupied bit of wall, far enough from a couple making out, and looked around for Marko or Flemm. I didn't see them, but the band was just about to go on and everyone was pushing toward the stage. I liked my spot, so I hung back. The lead singer—Crazy Steve Goof—started the show by chugging a can of Molson Ex and crushing it against his head. I felt my blood start to vibrate. The band attacked without mercy; a guy onstage was spitting fire. I stopped watching and joined the surge, closing my eyes and letting my brain ride the noise. My head fell into the rhythm and bobbed along, louder and madder. I wanted more.

Up near the stage, kids were thrashing. Every so often a body would fly over the top of the crowd in a flurry of fists and boots. I edged my way down to the speakers to get a better look. A guy got thrown out of the crowd and barrelled right into me, the impact sending a glow through my cells like a spreading bruise. Awash with adrenalin, I pushed him as hard as I could back into the crowd. I got kicked off my feet and chucked onto a couple of guys, one of whom I elbowed in the nose. He and I looked at each other as a trickle of blood escaped his nostril. He poked out his tongue and tasted the blood on his lip, then bellowed at me, the tendons in his neck stretched tight. I bellowed back. I got a fist in the ear and landed on the floor just outside the pit. A guy reached his hand out and helped me up. Then, once I was standing, he rammed his shoulder against mine, knocking me back into the pit. I came out of that night with bruises all over my ribs and the backs of both shirtsleeves torn, but I'll tell you, it felt good to hit—and to get hit. Talk about next phases of maturity: at last, my body was good for something.

✂

I started going to shows every chance I got. Hanging around Haller's, I got the first word about every new band and every show coming to town, and while the shows were good, for me, it was all about the pit. I'd wade in like a swimmer, close my eyes, and respond naturally to the shock of human touch.

I'd decided I was straight edge, like Henry Rollins—no drugs, no booze. Of course, I was only sixteen, so it wasn't exactly a choice, but it gave me a slight advantage. At my first Dayglo Abortions show, I was hanging out by the wall close to two drunk guys and a very drunk girl. All of a sudden, the girl leaned over and threw up at her feet, then slid to the floor into her vomit. The guys roared noiselessly in the chaos, pointing and laughing as she sat there slumped over, cross-legged, her kilt lifted to reveal the ripped crotch of her tights. Still laughing, they headed for the pit, one joyously head-butting the other on the way. I took a last look at the girl, sprawled out in the bit of space people were making for her, and followed them.

I only went after the bad ones. The rest of my joy in the pit came from the mutual violence cooked into the culture—it was an umbrella under which I could hurt and be hurt. I hit my own self less.

Although the shows brought some release, seeing Mitch and Spence thriving every day at school left me with a reserve of anger that, for want of another available target, I took out on my parents. I slammed doors and punched walls and stomped up and down the house, creating a tension I maliciously controlled, cranking it up whenever I wanted, just to see them react. Hurting my mother was easy because I'd gotten a head start, and her day-drinking was low-hanging fruit. With my dad, I weaponized our closeness. But my abuse had the unexpected result of pushing them closer as a couple. With a shared foe to battle, they started investing in their relationship, becoming friends rather than passive-aggressive adversaries. By the time my seventeenth birthday rolled around, the sad little pizza party they threw me felt more like a date of theirs I'd invaded, for all their cuddling. I brayed at the kitchen table about how I'd already filled out my Hair Academy application and only had to wait until I'd completed my high school diploma to send it in, making quite a show of how I wouldn't need them anymore and couldn't wait to be free of their bullshit. And if I was eager to be free of them, imagine how they longed for a moment's reprieve from me.

I came home one night to find them waiting up. I'd just been to a Subhumans show in a warehouse near the abattoir, and I walked in with a split lip and the reek of all the beer I'd knocked out of people's hands. My ears were ringing, and my knuckles were swollen, and there were a couple of idiots who wouldn't be calling me a dyke again anytime soon.

"Louise, this can't go on. Look at you," said my mother, her brow a capital M. "Are you bleeding?"

"Why does it have to be *bad*, Mom? Why can't this just be me? Why do I have to be the person *you* want me to be?"

"Is it? You?"

"Yes! I've never been happier!"

She pursed her lips.

"Have another glass of wine, Mom. I'm going to bed."

"Louise. Don't talk to your mother that way!"

"Oh, so you're taking her side now?"

"We both love you, and we're *both* very worried about you."

"You wouldn't be so worried if you'd gotten the boy you wanted, would you?"

"What?"

"Why else would you make me wear boy clothes and do boy stuff?" I wasn't even convincing myself—I just wanted so, so badly to fight.

My dad slapped his hands on his thighs. "*That's what you like!*"

Exhausted, I turned down the hallway, flicking the family portraits on my way, sending them one by one to the floor.

"LOU-*ISE*!"

"WHAT???!!!"

"Your. Mother. And. I. Are. Going. On. A. Trip."

I slunk back up the hallway to give them a good, long glare.

"Without me."

"Oh, so you'd like to come to Cape Breton with us?"

"Uh, *nooo*."

"No. We didn't think so. Well, you're old enough to stay by yourself, so we thought we'd give you a chance to show some responsibility."

"Boy, you must be pretty worried about me if you're leaving me here alone. *That* makes sense."

"Do you think you can handle it?"

"*Of course I can*. It'll be nice not to have you breathing down my neck for once."

On my bed, I tucked my knees to my chin, still wearing my beer-stinking coat. The terrorized townsfolk were fleeing the ogre.

As much as calm self-reflection clashed with my new way of being, I had to stop and wonder if all this was necessary. Melting down felt warranted every time they asked whether I'd eaten or where I was going, but deep down I knew how thin a mask this all was for my still-raw feelings about a certain carefree teenage boy, and I craved cheap relief. As for the teenage boy himself, I took no action at all, in spite of my prurient fantasies of feeding his penis into a meat grinder. I wasn't going to the principal—my parents would find out for sure what had happened if I did. And the police? It would certainly be the funniest report they'd receive that day. No, the abscess was mine to gestate, and it festered, ever-swelling, pushing against my rib cage like an extra heart.

✂

It was around nine at night, three days into my parents' vacation, when I got the call from the Cape Breton Regional Police. I was watching *Unsolved Mysteries*, eating Kraft Dinner on the couch, which I wasn't supposed to do. It would be days before I'd scrape those cemented noodles off the coffee table.

"Hon, are you still with me?" came the voice through the phone.

My parents' rental car had veered off the South Bar highway and pitched twenty metres down to the rocky shore below. They would have been killed on impact, or that's what the lady on the phone gently insisted. "They wouldn'a felt nothing, hon. They'd'a been gone."

Oh, but those last seconds. I squeezed my eyes shut and covered my face, imagining the earth speeding toward their windshield. The fear that must have gripped them. They were just normal people, living lives free of terror. If only they'd gotten a different daughter.

I teetered down the hall, catatonic, steadying my shoulder against the framed photos I'd knocked down so many times lately. I stopped and stared at one of me and my dad: we were on the front step, on my first day of school. Our ringleted heads were haloed, both of us squinting into the sun with hands raised to block the glare. It was the kind of photo most people wouldn't even keep, let alone frame. I picked it up and held it to my chest, kicking the baseboard with a foot I barely controlled. The next picture on the wall was of me looking furious aboard a paddleboat swan. I collected it, grabbing another and another as my shoulder slid along, until my arm met the bathroom doorframe, and I careened in. The sight of my mottled face in the medicine cabinet mirror sent my armful of photos clattering to the sink, and I moved in close to meet my fixed, dead eyes. The hot air from my nostrils fogged headlights in the glass—my heart surged, threatening to explode. Then, with my all hideous, frustrated rage,

I reared back and punched the mirror, splitting my face into jagged wedges that radiated from my knuckles, sparkling with the sting where the red seeped into the cracks.

I slowly lifted my hand, entranced by the blood that inched toward my forearm, the shocking brightness of colour. When I uncurled my fingers a thought-cancelling white light flared in my head, and when I flexed them a few more times I found I could forget I ever had parents, or that I'd demolished our relationship as a substitute for standing up to a snide, meaningless high school boy.

This tactic became standard whenever thoughts of them reared up. I could always find an opportunity for pain. A little worried about brain damage, I mixed it up from punching myself in the head, so I'd bang my elbows, wrists, shoulders, in ways I could hide. I preferred a solid impact to the sting of cutting and sought out edges and surfaces with the least give, like bathroom tiles, or brick, or concrete. The bruises themselves were a corollary reward atop the pain. I enjoyed the anticipation of the "up" days, while my wounds were building to their full breadth and severity, seeing just how bad they'd get. I liked them at their darkest, but also enjoyed the "down" days, when the red flecks of broken blood vessels stood out against the dissolving yellow patches.

I didn't have the skills to work through sadness or regret, but I could wield my own suffering against them, embedding the neglected core of my grief like a stone in my gullet.

1994-1997

THE COURT APPOINTED ME A guardian until I was eighteen to
make sure I finished school and didn't die, but they needn't
have bothered. One of the unlikely benefits of my frantic
mind was that, along with fretting counterproductively, it also
worried over practical things like getting assignments in on
time and maintaining access to food and shelter. My parents'
tiny estate had enough to keep me going through school, and
once I turned eighteen, the house was transferred into my
name. I started Hair Academy the week after I graduated,
devoting myself one hundred percent to my studies, never
once looking back at what I'd lost. There were bills to pay.
The only indulgence I allowed myself was in the pit, every
single chance I got.

Hair Academy had three programs: hairstyling, aesthet-
ics, and barbering. I only had to read the barbering program

description to know it was right for me. It was like a secret society, with traditions dating back centuries—it used to be the town barber who performed amputations, dental extractions, and leechings. The red stripe in the barber pole represented blood. And even though the curriculum included dry and hot-towel shaves, the academy's description stressed that the skills learned in barbering applied to *all* hair, not just men's.

I was the only girl in my class, and although my instructor often joked that my own hairstyle (much improved with my skills) and terrifying T-shirts might scare people off, he said I was a natural. I completed my courses, collected my diploma, and went looking for an establishment where I could fulfill my apprentice hours.

In barbershop culture, the client faces the door to greet the next man who enters. When I walked into Pascale's on Bloor Street, I got to watch all the faces first-hand as they fell mute with misgiving. I'd barely asked about apprenticing before a mustachioed barber, likely Pascale himself, declined with a pitying look. I'll hand it to them, they didn't really start laughing until I'd cleared the front door. But I keyed both cars in the customer parking spots anyway. I only had to get the same response a few times before I gave up and rented a chair at a Family Cuts in my neighbourhood.

And it was at that Family Cuts, one Saturday in May, that the cosmic ingredients of my destiny collided.

✄

I was pretending to cut the hair of a man named Mr. Junior, who came to see me every few weeks whether he needed it or not. This time he didn't, which was why I was pretending. I didn't get a lot of men's haircuts, because, of course, most men go to a barber. Mr. Junior could have gone to a barber too, but here's what he said when I asked why he didn't: "I prefer a girl." Just like that: *"I prefer a girl."* Mr. Junior was in his nineties and had only a sparse white fringe remaining around the back of his head, but he was a paying customer, which meant he got my full attention for the usual half hour like any other fifteen-dollar men's cut. Mrs. Junior had died a few years earlier, and Mr. Junior still didn't know what to do with his time—hence the haircuts. Otherwise, he walked, he said, and he napped. He liked to have a half cup of good, strong coffee before a nap, because he knew that at a given point while he was asleep it would kick in and he'd stand straight up in bed. "Might never wake up otherwise," he chuckled. It annoyed me that he was too pure-minded to recognize his erection innuendo, but really, he was talking about survival; I was the prude.

A nurse came to see him twice a week and told him jokes that he passed on to me. That day, it was:

"What's brown and sticky?"

I raised my eyebrows.

"A stick."

While his shoulders danced, I let my eyes wander to the mirror. There was a woman outside, sitting on the municipal beautification-initiative planter in front of the window, watching me open and close the scissors near Mr. Junior's head. I was six feet tall with a ginger tophawk, and passersby sometimes gawked at me through that window, but this was different. It was as if her gaze propelled me forward, somehow drawing a magic line between me and *womanhood*.

She might have been in her midforties, with pasta-fed, Mediterranean curves wrapped in a black snakeskin pencil skirt that looked like she'd been born in it and a Ramones T-shirt with the sleeves cut off. Her long black hair had a blue sheen, like Veronica's from the Archie comics, with a set of short bangs that extended behind her ears. Her sideburns were shaved to the skin, so as not to break the line of the bangs. Even for Toronto, she was breathtakingly cool. But what really struck me in the whole incredible package was her shoes. Each of her fishnet stockings ended in a men's lace-up black patent leather shoe. It was the 1990s, and you could wear combat boots with a dress, but these were *men's shoes*—not Doc Martens or some yellow-stitched imitation, but expensive leather shoes from an expensive men's store. I pictured her walking into a Yorkville men's boutique and commandeering an army of salespeople to find her the perfect pair of lace-ups to go with that Ramones T-shirt. The power she would wield, her command of their commissioned attention as they scrambled to satisfy her needs, pretending it was routine to fit beautiful women in men's dress shoes. She'd toppled the system.

We eyed each other as I ran a comb down Mr. Junior's

fringe, dusted off his nose, and swished the apron from around his neck, as though it contained hair. Then he put out his palm and I placed mine facing up inside it, against its papery warmth. Mr. Junior liked to tip me directly, convinced as he was that Ginette would steal it if he left extra at the cash. I made eye contact with the woman through the window as he reached into his pocket and pulled out the five-dollar bill. He laid it in my hand, resting his other on top, making a sandwich with his hands that contained my hand and the money. I liked Mr. Junior, but he had a way, during the hand-and-money sandwich, of searching my face for gratitude. It irked me, but it *was* five dollars. And the jokes were good.

I was tucking the bill into my tip jar when the woman from outside dropped into my chair.

"Can you do bangs?" she said, ignoring Ginette, who was holding the phone against her chest and had just called "Excuse me!" I pried my eyes from the woman to check if my next appointment was waiting. I didn't see anyone, so I waved back to Ginette that it was okay.

It was okay.

"Two millimetres off," said the woman. "No more."

"Spray?"

"Yes," she said. Then, seriously, "But don't get the rest wet. It gets curly." She glanced up at my hair and quickly considered and dismissed an acknowledgement. Her voice was solid, her delivery clipped. She smelled like cloves and carnations.

As I draped her, I noticed the soft pelt of black hair on her forearms and felt a flutter in my sternum. She had a timeless authenticity. She could have been Joan of Arc or Kathleen Hanna, from Bikini Kill.

"That last man," she said. "You didn't cut his hair at all."

"Ah, yeah." I masked her hair with my hand and spritzed her bangs with the Flairosol. "That's Mr. Junior. He comes to talk. And tell me jokes. But he's paying," I shrugged, "and if he wants a pretend haircut, then that's what I give him."

She closed her eyes as I combed her ends straight and painstakingly snipped. I inhaled the smell of cinnamon too, which I could only guess must have sprung from a divine well in her very pores.

"How do you know he wants you to pretend?"

During Mr. Junior's first visit, our eyes had met in the mirror just as I was recognizing how little hair he had, and I remembered their gentle plea. When I sprayed the naked pink top of his head, he relaxed and settled right in. I feel one of the reasons he kept coming back was the tacit agreement itself; you don't find those every day.

"Mr. Junior and I have an understanding," I said. "We don't need to talk."

"Mmhmm." She barely parted her lips as the infinitesimal trimmings sprinkled down her perfect nose. "I love not talking."

"Me too!" It's like she was reading my thoughts—or already knew them. I focused on the geometric perfection of her bangs, resisting the urge to stare at her mouth.

"You have great hair," she mumbled, eyes still closed. "Like Annabella Lwin."

"Who?"

"Annabella Lwin, from Bow Wow Wow."

"Hunh, I'll look her up." I made a mental note to broaden my musical knowledge and generally learn more things.

"Does everyone have hair like that at home?"

I paused so long that she opened her eyes, zeroing in on mine like a tractor beam.

"Um. No one's at home," I said, astonished to hear myself speak the words. "They're dead."

She held my gaze, stony irises ringed with black. I exhaled hard through my nostrils.

"Your parents?"

"They drove off a cliff. In Cape Breton."

"You're not even twenty, are you?" she asked, in a way that made me look forward to one day saying those words to a girl my age.

"I'm nineteen."

I held her bangs down with the comb and trimmed a last uneven strand, making sure they were absolutely straight. "Blowout?"

"Mmmm," she said, lost in thought.

I picked up the round brush and turned on the dryer. She shuddered under the apron and rolled her eyes shut ecstatically as I pulled her wet bangs between the bristles and concentrator nozzle.

When I was young, my dad used to blow-dry my hair. My mother would wash it while I was in the tub, and then after she'd towel-dried it she'd call "Oh Christof!" down the stairs—a little emasculating tool she used to help her watch him go off to work every day and come home smelling like women. You could see the vindication she felt in praising what a beautiful job he did, how he had such an eye for texture and volume. The thing is, he did. He could round-brush my curls into a Marlo Thomas flip that would last for days. Combined with my memories of the salon bonnet dryer, it's hard to overstate my love for hot, blowing air. I could not have felt more connected to this woman.

I clicked the switch and the roar subsided. She assessed her bangs in the mirror, pushing the backs of her fingers beneath their perfect curve. Her nails were short, her hands ropy with veins. She turned and faced me.

"So what are you, hardcore?"

"… Yeah."

"Do you want to make ten times the money you make here?" She didn't wait for an answer. "I own a salon where I think you'd fit right in. We're short a redhead. Interested?"

"I. Yes."

She stood and smoothed her skirt. "Good," she said, taking a card from her clutch and handing it to me. "I can already tell you're what I need."

The card said: *Hair for Men, Unit #12, Turcott Industrial Park, Mississauga.*

"Hair for Men? Is it a … a barbershop?"

"It's an experience." Then she added, "With hot-towel shaves."

I stared back at her. "I *love* shaving."

"I can tell." She held out her hand. "I'm Constance."

"I'm Louise," I said. I extended the tips of my fingers like a debutante at the cotillion, because at nineteen I'd still never been taught to shake hands.

"No," she said gently, taking my hand with her other one, pressing our palms firmly together. She fixed me with her grey eyes. "That's how you shake hands."

She tipped me a hundred dollars, stuffing the brown bill into my jar and completing a latent connection in my coral-coloured ambitions between womanhood, money, and me.

I rode home, my mind swimming laps between dreamy reverie and gnawing doubt. Ten times the money? Why an industrial park? And why only men? These were the questions a sensible young woman would ask as she skated home in the extended evening light. But the answers didn't matter. One of the by-products, I discovered, of not having parents was a freedom from moral obligation. I'd have trafficked heroin if that woman had asked. I had a fascination to feed, a sadness to forget, and my nineteen-year-old brain itched to know the kind of man who frequents an expensive men's hair salon in a remote Mississauga industrial park.

1997

CONSTANCE WASN'T ABOUT TO POACH another salon's stylist without notice ("There's a code"), so two weeks later I put on my Dayglo Abortions T-shirt and tied my hair in a high, curly knot, wove in some knitting needles, and headed off to my new job.

As I passed my skateboard in the hall I contemplated bringing it along, but the trip involved the subway and two buses. Giving one red wheel a spin with my finger, watching until it stopped, I decided to leave it.

I'd never been to Turcott Industrial Park, since I'd never needed laser-cut plastics or wholesale veterinary supplies. It was isolated. I grasped just how isolated only when the bus turned down yet another street lined with vinyl-sided factory buildings and I realized I hadn't seen a car or a pedestrian since we'd left the highway. The bus let me off at the monument sign in front of the nondescript grey block that contained Unit 12. Smokestacks huffed beyond the roofline. A transport truck sped by, then it all got very quiet. I paused at the end of the pebbled walkway before approaching the tinted glass door. Underneath the unit number was a brass plaque that said *Hair for Men* in a sensible serif font. I took a breath and pushed the buzzer. It buzzed back.

Inside, once my eyes had adjusted to the dim glow, the first thing to come into focus was the art deco pattern on the marble floor of white diamonds inside black diamonds. The walls of the sprawling reception area were papered in tasteful cream and gold stripes with ebony wainscotting, stretching up to a domed ceiling whose vastness didn't seem possible from outside. From its apex hung a frosted crystal chandelier that cast sparkling drops of light on the reception desk below. The squeak of my Vans echoed off the crown mouldings. On one side of the reception area stood an antique sofa, over which hung an enormous oil painting of three people sitting on a picnic blanket in a field—two clothed women, talking, and one nude man, looking over his shoulder at the viewer. On the wall opposite the painting was a long table laden with fruits and meats and breads, like a fancy brunch buffet.

A girl with blond hair cut on the half-inch setting of the clippers stepped out from behind the front desk. She was wearing a short-sleeved, fitted white smock that buttoned up one side, a long tartan kilt, and an excellent pair of fourteen-hole cherry-red Doc Martens.

"Louise." She smiled at me, and I noted a pierced lip and prominent canines. "I'm Sabrina."

Summoning Constance, I gripped her hand as firmly as she did mine, and we looked each other in the eye.

"Hi," I said.

"Your hair is great," she said.

"Thank you," I said. "Amazing boots."

I caught a look at the two of us in a gilt-framed mirror along the main wall so big I couldn't imagine how they'd have gotten it inside. I don't think I'd ever seen anything cooler than what she was wearing.

She swept an arm toward the long table. "Do you want a mimosa?"

"What's that?"

"Champagne and orange juice."

"Oh," I said. "I'm straight edge."

"Nice," she said. "Like Rollins. Well, there's a ton of juice and coffee. And fruit. Constance is very big on fruit."

I took a cup from the table and walked my fingers through the envelopes of herbal teas. Family Cuts this was not.

The front door opened and another girl came in, about the same age as me, holding a black bicycle helmet adorned with devil horns. She had tired eyes and brown hair in a short, blunt bob.

"Hey," the girl said, hand extended. "I'm Tori."

"Hey, I'm Louise." I firmly returned her handshake and held eye contact until she broke it to take off her coat, revealing a red velvet baby-doll dress barely covering a pair of white satin Adidas running shorts with green stripes down the sides. Who would even try an outfit like that?

"Tori plays clarinet," said Sabrina. "She's the shit."

"Aww ..." said Tori.

"No, we went to see her at a jazz club. She's unbelievable. You've got to come see her play."

"I really play classical," she said, "but I'm a hired gun for jazz."

"Wow." These girls weren't like anyone I'd met. I didn't know anyone who played any kind of wind instrument. And those shorts ...

A key scratched in the lock and the door opened to an enormous man with a black eye. He held a plastic bag of ice against the knuckles of his right hand. He was ginger like me, freckled, and his hair hung in dreadlocks down his back. Mythically handsome. When he noticed me, he lifted his wrapped hand, and a little water dripped from the bag.

"Oh," he said, "I'm so embarrassed. Today is your first day. I'm Augustus. I'd shake your hand, but ..."

The mass of his shoulders blocked all but a peek of a houndstooth suit locking the door behind him. As I nodded in acknowledgement, my eyes shot past him to Constance. In the two weeks since I'd met her, my imagination had distorted my memory of her to where she looked nothing like real life. I couldn't have made up anything this good: she wore a ripped Blondie T-shirt tucked tight into the houndstooth skirt of the suit, fishnets, and those same patent leather lace-ups. Her lips were glossy red. She came up behind Augustus and put her hand on his shoulder in a way I wasn't sure I liked.

"Augustus got in a fight," she said.

"Oh no," said Tori. "Auggie …"

"I know," he said. "I know."

"What happened?" asked Sabrina.

He hung his head and Constance said, "We were just picking up the champagne at the liquor store and we walked by these two idiots in the parking lot, and one of them says, 'Your girlfriend's got a fat ass.'"

I stifled the urge to gasp. How could anyone talk to her like that?

"So I said to the guy, 'I'd never disparage your ass. Why can't we treat each other with the same respect?' And the idiot says he wasn't talking to me. And then this other guy starts after Augustus, insisting that he should punch the first guy, like, 'What are you, some kind of pussy?' and 'You gonna let him get away with that?' and he kept on and on until …"

"I punched him," said Augustus.

"And then they piled on him, like they wanted to do in the first place." Constance turned to him. "Angel …" She touched his cheek just under his black eye. "Don't give them what they expect. It's the only way."

I looked at the floor.

"Anyway, he feels bad enough. Let's not make a thing of it." She turned to him, "Why don't you go bandage your hand."

She watched him lovingly as he disappeared down the hall. "He used to be a real scrapper when I met him. Couldn't turn down a fight, and because of the size of him, some fool was always there to provoke him. I didn't think we'd be able to make it work, but no lamb is so precious as the one who strayed from the flock and found his way back, right?"

Then she gave a sigh and turned to me. "Louise, welcome."

I was still reeling from the idea that someone would make a comment like that about her body—and that she didn't seem to care about it—as she came for me with both hands extended. One to shake my hand, and one to place on top. I grasped hers, I hoped not too greedily.

"Nice to see you," she said, pulling away before I did. "So now you've met the girls, and my boyfriend, Augustus."

"Oh," I said. "Yeah."

She crossed to the refreshments table. "Can I get you a mimosa?" she asked, making two.

"… Sure …"

She handed me a crystal flute and clinked hers against it. The champagne sort of ruined the orange juice, but I came around.

"Have the girls given you the tour?"

"I just got here."

"Lovely."

Sabrina returned from the back holding the hanger of a garment bag. "Here," said Constance, unzipping the bag and producing a fitted white smock like Sabrina's. She held it up to my chest and pulled it down around my waist. "This should be perfect on you. Lord, I'd never get away with those pants. Army surplus?"

"Navy," I said stupidly.

"You're blessed," Constance said, folding the smock over her arm. "Let's go see your booth." She picked up her drink and I followed.

Down the hall, there were four heavy black doors, two on either side, and a washroom at the end, a cherub-bedecked fountain visible just inside its entrance.

"Wow," I said. "This is nice. I've never seen a salon like this."

"Well, it is a little different."

"Telling me."

Pointing to the doors one at a time, she said, "This is Sabrina, Tori, my office, and this is you." She opened the last door for me. "I'll be right across from you."

I walked into a room with a checkerboard floor, decorated by the same taste that would pair a houndstooth suit with a Blondie T-shirt. The room wasn't a booth; it was a small, beautiful, mahogany-walled private salon. On the back wall was a hair-washing sink and chair with an antique stool, next to a big closet that held a push broom and long-handled dust-pan. A gilt-framed mirror faced a red leather upholstered chair with a hand crank and a shoeshine pad. It looked old. And expensive. From a hook to the left of the mirror hung a vintage stainless-steel hair dryer; from the right-hand hook, a suspended basket with four different sizes of Wahl clippers. The counter held a blue Barbicide jar full of combs, and an alcohol-filled one with straight razors, a row of pomades, a duster, a dish of talc, and a folded towel, on top of which sat three different sizes of scissors.

"Are those ...?"

"Mizutanis," she said.

"Holy."

Mizutanis were made of Damascus steel, the same metal used to make samurai swords. Constance picked up a pair and handed them to me. I had never been in the same room as a pair of Mizutanis, let alone slid my fingers through their rings. They were so light and clean, more like ice than metal. I placed them reverently back on their towel.

A high shelf to the right of the mirror held a big silver bell.

"What's that for?"

"Augustus," she said, setting her mimosa on the counter. She gestured for me to sit. The chair wheezed out a little air from the corner seams beneath me.

"Sometimes, Louise, people get the wrong idea about what goes on here. You try to innovate, you try to provide something that, when you come right down to it, is essential to us as humans, and certain vulgar assumptions invariably get made. If any man asks what services we offer, other than revolutionary cut, shave, and style, you tell him nothing. We do hair. Anyone gives you trouble of any kind, you ring the bell." She leaned in gravely. "Got it?"

"Hair," I said.

"Just hair." She nodded. "Okay, so, it's two hundred dollars, cash, at the end of the day. You keep all your tips. Catering brings in breakfast and lunch, so you don't have to worry about that ... Are you vegetarian?"

"No."

"Good. Tori, Sabrina, and Augustus are, so you and I are the only carnivores. Delorme's Meats, two streets up, brings us some charcuterie that I am absolutely helpless for. Have you ever had bresaola?"

I shook my head again.

"It's paper-thin cured beef, so supple it feels like you're touching your tongue against your own tongue. I'll be glad to have someone to eat it with."

"Gool," I said. Jesus ...

"So you've got your towel warmer, razors, a Latherizer— it's a throwback, but it heats up quick and who doesn't love hot lather?" She pushed the lever of the device and a blob of hot foam landed in her palm. She reached out and held it up to my nose.

"Men are delicious, aren't they?" she said, massaging the blob into her hands and taking a big sniff.

"Sure ..."

She laid a fingertip on the handle of the chair. "Have you used a Paidar?"

"The chair?"

She gave me a vigorous demonstration of the hydraulic

lever, into which she threw her entire back, then showed me the finer points of the design, like the loop where you could hang your razor strop, the adjustable headrest, and the deep recline.

"You can keep your things in the closet here," she said, graceful arm extended, "and let me know if you need anything at all. You've got Richard at ten thirty, who's very eager to meet you. We don't get a lot of new girls. You'll love Richard. He's the vice principal at Parklawn High. He's been coming here for years."

"Okay …" I said.

"We're all so excited to have you here, Louise. Thank you. So, try on your smock. I'll go open things up, and we'll see you in a few."

"Totally," I said.

After she'd left, I turned in a full circle, admiring the room. I'd never been close to things this nice. I wondered why you'd have a salon with private rooms, and why Richard was so eager to meet me, but other thoughts—of bresaola, of Mizutanis, of two hundred dollars cash at the end of the day—quickly stole my attention.

I hung my coat in the closet and looked around for cameras before taking off my T-shirt, huddling my back to the room just in case. I slid the sturdy cotton smock on over my bra and buttoned it across my shoulder and down the left side. The bottom was reinforced with two wide pockets that acted sort of like holsters for styling tools. The fit was snug, but comfortable—the buttons didn't even pull across my rack—and made me look both more feminine and more *surgical* than I'd ever looked. Constance had somehow gotten my size exactly right, which even I couldn't do.

I scanned the tools at my station, picked up the six-and-a-half-inch Mizutanis, opening and closing them in the perfect silence of their hinge.

The antique hair dryer made a deep, friendly *vrrrrrrrrr-rrrrrrrrrrrrrrrrrrrrrr*. The tone and register of the drone varies from unit to unit, depending on the motor, design, ventilation. The older ones tend toward lower registers, and give a deep, full-body shudder you don't get from the modern, high-pitched screamers. The old ones get into your teeth. I've always preferred the baritones. I blew the nozzle up under my smock, then under my arms one at a time. It was almost ten thirty. I drank the rest of my mimosa, which made my head just fuzzy enough to kill the last of my nerves. I laid my hands on the counter, leaned forward, and looked myself in the face.

"All right?" I asked my reflection.

✂

In the reception area, Sabrina and Tori were both smocked, poring over the appointment book, drinking espresso.

"That's perfect on you," said Tori when I walked in.

"Oh nice," said Sabrina. "Have you tried lifting your

arms? Lift your arms." The three of us lifted our arms. "It's so comfortable, eh? It doesn't even pull up."

"They're so great," said Tori. "Constance orders them custom from Italy."

Tori turned the appointment book around to face me. "Look," she said, "you've got Richard at ten thirty. Richard was my first too. You'll love him."

There was so much to ask, but the longer I went without asking, the less I felt I could. The column under *Louise* in the book was a list of men's names: Richard, Virgil, Rakesh, Layne …

"So … it's a cool place to work?" I asked.

"Oh, it's amazing," said Tori. "I could never go back to regular hair."

"Me neither." Sabrina nodded.

"What makes it so great?"

"The men!" they said together.

"What about the men?"

"They're just the best," said Tori.

I narrowed my eyes.

"Don't worry," said Tori. "Just, if anyone asks, it's only hair, right?"

"Yeah," I said. "I got that."

"And don't discuss money," said Tori. Sabrina shot her a look. She lowered her voice. "I mean, even out here. Because …" She pointed to the chandelier, then all around the ceiling.

"Okay …"

"It gets normal," said Sabrina. "Like anything."

Tori leaned in and, whisper-excited, said, "Ohhh, you're going to love it."

From the hallway came the buttery eruption of Constance's laugh as she and Augustus appeared. He had taken off his coat and was wearing a tight green Fresca T-shirt, the sleeves straining over his freckled biceps. It was very hard not to stare—he was *so* handsome. The green of his shirt with the flaming ropes of his hair … When I was a kid, I had a Pulsar: Ultimate Man of Adventure doll—the only doll I ever owned. Pulsar had a clear plastic chest you could see his organs through, and a button on his back that activated his heart and lungs. Augustus reminded me of Pulsar. He was just so … immediate. As he walked past Constance, she reached after him and patted his ass.

"Oh Louise, look at you," she said. "You're perfect."

The door buzzed and she clapped her hands. "Here we go!"

Tori crossed to the buffet and started shovelling ice into a martini shaker. She reached for a bottle as Sabrina picked up the phone and hit the button. A bespectacled man with sandy brown hair entered; he was wearing a beige corduroy jacket and brown pants. He walked right over to Constance and shook her hand. As he did, I got a look at the back of his head, which was slightly flattened.

"Thanks for squeezing me in, Constance. I really appreciate it."

"Pleasure to see you, Richard." She stepped back to present me. "This is Louise."

"So, so great to meet you," said Richard, coming forward with the same sincere handshake.

"You too," I said, returning it. So much handshaking.

Tori poured something like pale-red Kool-Aid into a martini glass and held it out to Richard, touching his elbow with familiarity. "Ooh, thanks," he said. A smile passed between them.

"All right," said Constance, putting her hand on the small of his back and leading him away. I turned to Sabrina.

"We give them some time to get settled," she said. "It's a shock coming here from the outside. Give him about five minutes, then knock."

"Why is it ... like this?" I asked finally.

"How do you mean?" asked Sabrina.

"Like, all of it." I gestured around the room. "The private rooms—and what's he drinking?"

"A cosmopolitan. Do you want me to make you one?"

"No, I ... just ... why is it so different?"

"It's for them." She shrugged. She picked up a slice of pineapple from the catering table. "I wish they were all like Richard," she said. "You won't have any problem with him. Some of the non-regulars though ..." She rolled her eyes.

"What?" I said. "What about them?"

"Oh, they just don't know how to behave. You'll almost never have to call Auggie, but it's a good thing he's here."

As she said it, Augustus appeared.

"What's good?" he asked.

"Not calling you," said Sabrina.

He exhaled heavily through his nose. "Yeah," he said, and paused for a few beats, looking at his hands.

I didn't want to like Augustus, but he was undeniably nice. Constance wouldn't have dated a jerk. Women must have stopped to stare at him all the time. Jerk or not, as a point of personal pride, I didn't want him coming to my aid. I'd be the one who never touched that bell.

"Hey," I said, nodding to his hand. "I would have punched him too."

"Aww," he said. "Nothing got solved. And I hate letting her down."

"But you're security," I said. "You're supposed to hit people."

"Not like that," he said. "That's just a lack of imagination. I don't know what it was about those guys. They set me off."

"Well, I think you did the right thing," I said. "Those guys sounded like shitbirds."

"Shitbirds." He chuckled half-heartedly, climbing the few steps to what looked like a high chintz upholstered lifeguard chair with a canopy overtop and a reading light inside. He crossed his legs campfire style and picked up a copy of *The Golden Notebook* from the end table.

Constance appeared from the hallway. "Okay," she said excitedly. "You're all set."

"Knock 'em dead," said Augustus. "But not actually." Something my dad would have said.

"Thanks." I didn't want to make a big deal about it, but their parental vibe was strong, and I felt compelled to make them proud.

The closed door loomed ominously as I craned my neck up at the high, moulded frame, like Alice in Wonderland. I knocked.

"Come on in," said Richard.

First thing I noticed when I walked into the room was him, sitting in the shampoo chair, sipping his cosmopolitan. The next thing I noticed, because it was almost touching my arm as I stood in the doorway, and because I'd only seen a few in my life, was the hot-pink edge of a fifty-dollar bill poking out from under the security bell. I closed the door and stood with my back against it.

"So …" I said, focusing on him and not the bill. "How much are you looking to get off?" I winced.

"Oh, just a trim," he said casually. "Say about an inch?"

"Sure."

I crossed the black-and-white tiles and came to stand beside him at the sink. His hair spun out clockwise like a drainage spiral from his crown before plunging down the steep incline of his head. When I pulled my fingers through it, it felt like the down of a baby chick. An inch was barely a haircut, but I knew to never question a customer's request— unless I felt they might be a threat to themselves and needed someone to step in. But he seemed so pleased to be there, the haircut didn't seem to matter.

"Shave?" I asked.

"I can't say no to the Latherizer." He interlaced his fingers over his belly.

I hadn't shaved anyone since school, but you never forget the intrinsic elements of beard softening and directional stroke. For me, though, shaving was all about the moment at the end—after concealing a man with foam and slowly revealing his face to him inch by inch—when he recognizes himself in the mirror and sees the face he's always had. *There* he is.

I draped the towel behind Richard's neck, and as I eased him into the sink, he relaxed so his head dangled over the lip. I had a moment's concern about his spinal column, but his face stayed so peaceful.

"How's it going so far?" he asked.

"I think it's going okay," I said, testing the water temperature. "There's fruit."

"It's nice, eh?" he said. "I'll tell you something, I'd live here if I could. There's just nowhere else like it. I hope it's a good place to work."

"It's cool so far," I said. "I love my smock."

"You can put so much in those pockets," he said, eyes on the ceiling. "Women's pants—and I say this without accusation—but they're ridiculous. No pockets. And if they do have pockets, they're too shallow to even hold a set of keys."

"I know!"

"I can put my wallet in my front or back pocket," he continued. "Men's pockets are designed deep enough to hold your whole hand, for one, but also the pants themselves aren't meant to be worn so tight that I can't fit an extra inch and a half thickness without ruining the way they look." He reached down and easily pulled out his wallet, held it up, then returned it to his pocket, where it took on a presence.

"We're supposed to carry *purses*."

"In order to hold all the makeup we insist you buy in order for us to find you attractive—so long as you don't *look* like you're wearing makeup."

"Right. You're supposed to have all the money and we're supposed to trick you into thinking we're pretty so you might give us some of your money."

"That's it."

I laughed. I wouldn't normally have prattled on like this, but there didn't seem to be the usual gendered barrier between us. It was like we already knew each other. Yet there was nothing special about him. He was just a regular man. Like my dad.

I rubbed a shampoo that smelled like root beer and leather between my palms. He breathed in deeply and closed his eyes as I brought the shampoo to his temples.

"I don't know why women don't just buy men's pants," I said. "I do."

"Louise," he started as I lathered, "you rejected conventional femininity the moment you took a razor to your head.

In your decision to chuck the norm, you've taken on risks—of mockery, of exclusion. There are rewards that come with those risks, and one of those rewards is that no one expects you to wear pants with pockets you can't use. It must be liberating. It's other women who suffer."

"Mm," I said. I had to really pay attention to what I was doing and didn't speak for the rest of the wash and condition. I brought him back to the chair with his towel-wrapped head and dressed him in the neck strip and cape. His head inched higher as I pushed the hand brake forward the way Constance had shown me, then back, then forward again. The hydraulics were smooth, but you definitely had to reef on the thing.

"I'll tell you what's not liberating," I said, tapping out a comb from the Barbicide jar. "It's that no matter how unconventional I am, or that I dress like a dude, my body still gets stared at and commented on, like that's what it's *there* for. It turns me into something … that I never meant to be. And I don't even get a say! All I can do is get mad! It must be amazing being a man, having a body that belongs to you and not everyone else. I hope you never forget how lucky you are."

"I never do." He reached out from beneath the cape for a sip of his drink, then replaced it on the counter. "I'd be mad too. It must be infuriating."

"It's bullshit."

"It *is* bullshit."

I snipped thoughtfully for a while. It's a challenge when someone has a head shape that can't be fixed. I decided to do a little extra tapering at the nape of his neck, because it would make the back look more rounded.

"Do you like cosmos?" he asked.

"You know, I'm not sure. I don't drink, or … I haven't for very long."

"Oh," he said. "Do you want to try some of mine?"

"That's okay. But thank you."

"I hate beer," he said. "I don't like the taste, and it makes me feel full. A cosmo is vodka, lime, triple sec, and cranberry juice. Well, it's mostly vodka, which is almost completely tasteless and odourless, but you know it's there. A cosmo is tart, strong, and you don't feel full afterward. Now, my wife, she likes beer. Loves it. We went to Rome years ago, and while we were there, we sat on a terrace near the Trevi Fountain. It was sunny. My wife ordered a beer. I ordered an Aperol spritz, which comes in a wine glass and is typically considered a ladies' drink. When the waiter took our order, he looked confused. It's just a little outside a meaninglessly rigid norm, right? But when he came back, he handed me the beer and my wife the Aperol spritz. We laughed as we slid them across to each other, but he just handed us our bill without looking up. We didn't see him again. We paid inside. When I come here, there's no goddamn fuss about my drink. I'll have one at ten thirty in the morning for the social acceptance alone. But today, I have to suspend three students, so I could use the extra courage. Teenage boys …,"

"Ugh, they're the worst," I said, tilting his head with my thumb. "They're disgusting. What did they do?"

He sighed. "One of them lifted a girl's skirt and they took a picture. In the hall. The others dared him to do it."

"Fuckers," I said. Then, "Sorry."

"These kids ..."

I stopped cutting. "I'm sorry, I ..."

He looked into my eyes in the mirror. "They're at such a fragile point, Louise. They were just little boys a short time ago, and it was okay for them to have feelings and get sad and want to be held ... You can still see hints of it in them sometimes. But by their age, the world has already started seducing them with its tasteless, odourless promises. They don't feel it happening, and they don't have any idea what they're losing in the bargain. All they see are the perks: physical dominance, higher pay, respect, the presumption of competence ..."

"The perks look pretty good."

"Oh, they are."

I dusted off his neck and tilted him back for his shave. I couldn't imagine feeling any sympathy for teenage boys, not after my own experience, but it struck me then that Richard was a teacher, and he was showing me perspective, a tactic I'm sure he employed with his students.

A blast of steam escaped from the towel cabinet when I opened the door, and I shook out a towel a few times to cool it down. He sighed as I draped the lower half of his face, made a roll at the bottom to tuck in his chin, then wrapped the towel around his nose, folding the excess at forty-five degrees from each side to cover his eyes. The shining tip of his nose poked out the end of the towel package as I pressed gently with my fingertips. Standing behind him, I watched myself in the mirror holding his immobilized face. The likeness to a mummy or a bandaged hostage is inevitable, but even so, a hot-towel wrap is one of the kindest things you can do for someone.

"How come you're not like that?" I asked, undraping his pinkened face.

"Like what? A teenage boy?"

"No …" I said. "Like a … regular man."

"Oh, I'm as damaged as the rest of us, Louise, but I do what I can. At least I'm aware of the poison—or I try to be. My wife never lets me forget. When you really love a woman, you don't forget."

"That sounds nice." I massaged his jawline with a pre-shave cream. After another hot towel, I pressed the Latherizer lever and filled my palm with the citrusy foam. The room was alive with a musky aroma—it lightened my head and sent crystal clear thoughts to the surface. Richard tilted his chin up in thoughtful anticipation of the badger bristles, but also, I realized, to listen. I lathered in little circles, the scratch of the brush and the slide and pop of the cream making their own little song.

"In high school," the words tumbled out, "I, um, so really just a few years ago, I got uh, well, ungh—I let someone— someone did some things to me and I wish they hadn't, and now I can't stand the idea of anyone touching me. I haven't even been to the doctor."

"Jesus," mumbled Richard.

Shaking a razor from the jar and pulling the skin taut over his cheekbone, I started on his left side, each short, light stroke like the sound of tearing a grapefruit rind.

"And I think about that guy—not every day, but a lot of days—and I think about killing him. Violently." I wiped a strip of foam on the towel over his shoulder. "There's nothing to be done—it's not bad enough to do anything about. It's just not bad enough ... And I'll never be free of him, this meaningless person. Every time the memory bubbles up, there he is. I'm sure he's out there, completely unbothered. I doubt he's given me a second thought. But I get him forever. For the rest of my stupid life ..." I gave his chin a final swipe, found an oil on my stand that smelled like licorice and lime, and gave him a second, closer shave to catch the few stray whiskers. As I finished his right jawline, clear as day, I saw a teardrop slide down his temple into his ear. I tilted him upright.

"I'm sorry, Louise," he said after a moment. "I'm sorry we didn't fix this before you came along."

I rested my hand on the back of the chair before moving it to his shoulder and giving it a squeeze. He brought his hand up to cover mine. Its warmth caught me up short. It might have been the smell of the styling products, or the mimosa before, or the fact that I couldn't remember the last time I'd hugged someone, but I wrapped my other arm around him and brought my head down onto his shoulder. He reached up and clasped my forearm, awkwardly stretched across him, resting his cheek on my arm.

When I whisked off his cape at the end, I was shaking.

"You okay?" he asked.

I nodded. Still seated in the chair, he reached out his hand. I grabbed it with both of mine.

"Thank you, Louise," he said quietly. "I'll see you out front."

Trying to look as though I'd expected this, I smiled and half bowed, and backed through the door.

Out in the hall, I held the doorknob and exhaled, feeling euphoric and terrified, grateful and embarrassed. I looked around at the other closed doors as I staggered away from mine, pausing in front of Tori's to listen. All I could hear was Baroque music piped through from the lobby, which felt like it was a mile away. When I finally reached it, Constance was lying on the antique sofa, reading Herman Hesse's *Steppenwolf*. Flemm had had a tattered copy that sat behind the counter at Haller's, so named for its hero. He'd told me it was the only book a person needed to read because it affirms our rejection of conformity. I'd read it three times.

At the sound of my approach, Constance marked her page. I tottered like a fool in front of her, not knowing whether to start with *Steppenwolf* or Richard. She placed the book beside her and stood, raising her hands so they hovered near my sides. I looked into her face, and she began to nod, touching my forearms. Holding back the pressure in my throat, I gestured.

"I've … read that." God, she smelled good.

"Okay …"

I gave my head a shake. "Jeez."

"It's okay, Pup," she said. "It can be overwhelming. Have some melon." She guided me to the fruit tray. When she put a hand on the small of my back, I nearly screamed, my senses were so overloaded with root beer and lime and Richard and tiny pockets and *Steppenwolf*. Her touch was like an accelerant.

"Thank you." I picked up a cantaloupe slice. I chewed, I breathed, I pointed to the couch. "That book is amazing."

She smiled. "Makes you feel so much less alone, doesn't it? When you feel like two parts of a human—one that's made for the world and one that's not."

"Yes!" How was it possible she knew me so well?

"Until you grow up and realize that life isn't so simple. There's more than human and animal in us; there are thousands. We are thousands. That's what Hesse was really trying to say. I first read this when I was your age, but it has a whole different meaning for me now. Harry is contemplating a life lived and the onset of its final act. It's a book of transition. I pick it up from time to time to better understand the early impulse in a young man to believe he's either a brooding misanthrope or a tool of the bourgeoisie. The danger for men in particular is in accepting society's demand that they be only one thing, and so never realizing the full potential of all their glorious moral and emotional complexity."

"Men are complex?"

"What did you just see in there?"

"That's ... just one man."

Constance gestured over her shoulder at Augustus, sitting in his canopied perch. "What about Augustus?"

"You have to admit ..." he said, looking up from his book.

"Okay, that's two."

"Two is a good start."

Their continued parental vibe reminded me of my own parents and was starting to make me sad, so I stuffed another slice of melon in my mouth. I never wanted this floaty feeling to end.

Richard emerged from the hallway, straightening his tie.

"How'd our girl do?" asked Constance sunnily. She crossed over to the reception desk.

"She did a great job." Richard was checking himself out in the multiple reception area mirrors. "It's like she rounded out the back of my head. And I've never had a closer shave. She went over twice—I haven't had that since I was in Milan."

He shook my hand firmly. "Thanks so much, Louise. It's a heck of a shave."

"Thanks," I said. Then, without letting go of his hand, I abruptly added, "Good luck expelling those boys."

Richard nodded. "We'll see what happens. It's a sad, infuriating situation, but I'll try my best to help them understand."

I felt the same powerless frustration that used to precede my knocking down the hall photos. I don't know what I thought I was accomplishing, like I could possibly have some kind of influence over a few teenage boys I'd never meet, but I couldn't stop myself. "They'll understand they're not allowed to come back to school because they're assholes."

"I know, I know. But imagine them without an education, Louise." Richard slid back into his perspective mode. "I mean, what do we do with them? Where do we put them once we decide they can't be redeemed?"

"Ice floe?" I suggested. "Labour camp? Devil's Island? Somewhere there are no girls?"

"Okay," said Constance conclusively. I was still holding Richard's hand.

He turned to her. "She's wonderful," he said.

"She is," said Constance. "We may need to keep an eye on some of her more sanguinary tendencies is all." She winked at me, sending my already bursting soul heavenward.

As I headed back to sweep up my booth, I ran "Sanguinary Tendencies" over in my mind, declaring it the best band name ever, and resolving to keep an eye on mine if Constance said so. You didn't see her hitting people—I bet she'd never thrashed in a mosh pit. I doubt she had that impulse at all, which made it seem childish in me. The way everything else about her made me feel.

I wondered at the promise of the day's list of clients. I pictured Richard addressing Mitch and Spence in a classroom, sitting on the corner of his own desk, hands stacked atop his thigh. In my fantasy, he was leaning in, saying, "You can't imagine what you're missing. I mean, they're a whole half of the population." Mitch was rolling his eyes, snickering, and Spence was drumming his desk, not paying attention. And then, all of a sudden, I slammed open the classroom door, the wired-glass window shattering from the force. Spence looked on helplessly as I grabbed Mitch by the throat, lifting him up out of his desk so his feet kicked the air. He made froggy noises with his crushed windpipe the whole way across the room until I lifted him onto a meathook, severing his spine—like Leatherface in *The Texas Chainsaw Massacre*—and he gurgled and bled out. Spence fled, wailing out into the hall, and spent the rest of his earthly time crouched in the corner of some small room, rocking back and forth, forever tormented by what he'd watched me do to his friend. As I joined Richard, sitting beside him on the desk, he handed me a cosmopolitan.

My outward impulses would be easier to control than the fantasies that flickered into my mind at the slightest provocation, instinctually channelling my urges. It was as natural as breathing.

The door to my booth was open and I could see the cape draped over the chair inside. As I crossed the threshold, the security bell stopped me. Under it, a brown bill had replaced the pink one. I eyed it and scanned the room again for cameras before pulling it out. It was crisp and new, straight from the bank. One hundred dollars. I studied Sir Robert Borden's sober face, turning the bill over in my hands before folding it up and sliding it in the pocket of my smock.

1998–2008

THEY WEREN'T ALL SWEETHEARTS, OF COURSE. Regulars were our mainstay, but every so often we'd get someone who'd heard the wrong thing and come for the wrong reason. I dealt with a few of them early on—without needing to call Augustus. My first was a wealthy, white-haired man named John. Constance flagged him in the book during her morning review. *John* was a name to keep an eye on. When he arrived, she introduced herself with her usual handshake; he returned it while staring at her chest. My eyelid quivered. She turned and gave me a barely perceptible shake of her head. When she led him down the hall, I glanced up at Augustus on his perch. He gave me the same stiff shake of his head.

John was in his sixties and wouldn't be hard to take down. A check of my knuckles revealed fresh, pink, almost completely healed scars. I hadn't hit anyone in months. The last time I'd tried to hit a guy at a show, I found I'd lost the heart. It was a relief.

Constance returned from delivering John to my booth and touched my arm. "All right, Pup, it's just hair. Just hair. These happen sometimes."

I gave her a brave nod. Not that I'd ever have called him, but I did take some comfort in knowing that Augustus was just down the hall, reading Doris Lessing.

When I knocked, John said, "Yep." I noted the problems right away—he was in the Paidar, smiling with anticipation, his suit jacket hanging in the closet with his expensive silk tie rolled up and tucked into a side pocket. The top two buttons of his shirt were undone, the collar pushed open. Most importantly, there was no pink bill tucked under the bell.

I smiled and patted the Mizutanis in my pocket. "So, what are you looking for today?"

"Welp, what are you offering?"

"I'd say you could use a standard trim, no shave—you seem to have just done that yourself."

"All right then." He winked. "Standard trim, no shave it is."

I led him to the sink and draped him. As I leaned him back, he was a little resistant. I took a moment to weigh his head in my hand. Eight pounds, the standard human head. Heavy to carry around in a bag, but lighter than a bowling ball—or so my dad had claimed.

John sat through the shampoo and conditioning, but once I'd towel-dried his hair and tried to wrap his head, he waved me off. "Naw, it's fine. C'mon." He crossed to the chair and looked over his shoulder impatiently. The flow of blood to my head darkened my vision.

I hesitated with my hand on the brake, then I unlocked it and gave it three sharp cranks, jolting him a little each time. He half laughed.

"Powerful little lady, aren't you?"

I smiled. He was good for a minute or two as I combed his hair and defined his natural part, but when I came around to his right side with the scissors, he stretched a finger out from under the cape and brushed it against my arm.

"Oops, better stay under there," I said, playfully making a snip-snip motion with the scissors. He grinned, like I was finally coming around, then reached down with the same hand to touch my pant leg. A white bolt of pure exhilaration sped from my thigh to my hand. I grabbed the headrest and wrenched it back so John was lying flat. My senses were so lit I thought I'd burst out laughing. I clamped his arm and brought the scissors to his eye. "If you touch me one more time," I said, "I will cut your fucking face off."

He looked at his feet for the rest of a very terse haircut and tipped a sheepish ten dollars, but when I shook his hand at the end, it was with genuine gratitude to know how close to the surface lay my primal instinct. How right it felt. How mine. I should have paid *him*.

What I wasn't expecting, two months later, was to see John's name again, with the same phone number, in my appointment list. Augustus said he'd turn him away at the door, but I said to let him come back. I didn't think he'd start trouble.

This time, when I walked into the room, he was sitting in the Paidar, clearly deep in thought.

"So?"

"I, uh," he said, "I guess I got my wires crossed last time and I was thinking something that wasn't right."

"All right."

"But ... it stayed with me. No one's ever looked at me the way you did, and I guess I saw myself how you saw me, and ... I ..." He tapped his fingertips together in his lap. "You know, I have a daughter your age, and she gets on me about the stupid things I say because I'm an old man. I know things are different now. But habits are hard to break, especially when I think I'm paying a lady a compliment. Anyway, I'm working on it. Kelly will love me no matter what, but when I thought about the way you looked at me ... Well, it stayed with me."

I said nothing.

"So I wanted to come back, for one thing, to show you I'm not a degenerate. And for another, because I'm about to retire and I've worked my whole life in banking where it's not allowed—for my daughter, and for you—I'd like to get my hair shaved up the sides like yours with a sort of pompadour, like Porter Wagoner. Do you know who that is?"

"No."

"He used to sing with Dolly Parton. They sang some of the prettiest songs."

"I'd love to, John."

"My name isn't John, you know. It's actually Burt."

"Mine's actually Louise."

Burt tipped me twenty dollars for that haircut, and for every one after that. It wasn't a Sir Robert, but I was happy to make the exception. He was my first convert. We maintained his undercut and pompadour for about four years, until it was just wisps. The day he came in and asked me to finally shave the lot, I offered him one last wash.

"I'm gonna miss that shampoo," he said, his voice breaking.

I laid my hand on his shoulder. "It's okay," I said. "You can do that here."

✂

I was undeniably softening. My musical preferences were veering artier: the impossible romance of Nick Cave, the operatic savagery of Diamanda Galás, the wickedness of Lydia Lunch. I was going to the repertory cinema all the time, and not just when *The Evil Dead* was playing. There was so much to consume, created by minds as harassed and horrified by the norm as Rollins's, and even he was going arty. Besides, it was hard to maintain my hardcore attitude when I wasn't feeling quite so angry anymore.

I sold my parents' house; I bought a condo and a sensible Volkswagen Passat and hired an investment adviser, which made it virtually impossible to hang out with the Haller's guys anymore. My conventional choices didn't fit with their conventions.

I'd picked up a few valuable lessons in my time with them, most notably in the area of law enforcement; one thing I knew was how to spot an undercover cop. Hardcore shows were always getting busted for drugs, underage drinking, assault—you name it. Law enforcement was the enemy and was always nearby. Sometimes they tried to infiltrate, to find out about the parties going on afterward so they could bust them up, that kind of thing. Marko had told me the surest way to spot a cop was that they'd be asking questions. Once you're part of the scene, you don't ask; you just find out. Anyone skulking around wanting to know where the party was, we gave them the address of a Tim Hortons in Regent Park.

My first cop at Hair for Men was Neil: late thirties with a barber fade a week and a half old. So obvious. Neil didn't ask for a drink and didn't smile when he shook my hand. Moreover, the first thing he wanted to know about was the one thing I'd been told not to discuss. He phrased the question in the precise words Constance had used.

"So, other than hair, what services do you offer?"

By then I knew perfectly well what services I offered. I was a total pro.

"Services?"

"You know, other than, like, hair and shaving?" He gestured vaguely.

"Sir," I said, "we're a salon. We offer revolutionary cut, shave, and style. I don't know what you have in mind, but if you're looking for anything else, this might not be the place."

That's when he smiled.

I ran my hands through his hair. "It doesn't look like you need much off."

"Yeah," he said. "Maybe just a shave? With the hot towels and the lime stuff?"

"Uh-huh," I said.

"Uh-huh," he said back, glad the business was out of the way so that he could get on with talking about his garden. He told me about the chicks and hens running roughshod over his lupins and how he enjoyed the music of Crowded House for Neil Finn's sensitive songwriting. He liked to sing along to it in the car. He only slipped once during that first visit, while describing the arrangement he'd planted around the gazebo.

"Gazebo …" I laughed.

"Yeah," he said. "The guys at the station don't let me forget about that one."

I caught his eye in the mirror.

"And what do you do, if I may ask?"

He hesitated a split second, then gave me a look where his eyes told me not to believe him, and said, "Radio. I'm in radio."

I saw Neil every so often over the years, along with a few other cops—they couldn't just keep sending the same one to ask the same question. We'd obviously caught on, but I think that's what Neil liked. The arrangement meant he got a hot-towel shave in a posh men's salon and didn't have to ruin the lives of a few young women. We'd developed a sort of routine, since he was technically required to question me every time.

"So tell me about these extra services," he'd say in a sort of W. C. Fields voice.

"Sir," I'd respond primly, "we are a hair salon."

One time, out of nowhere, he asked me if I'd ever been to Cape Breton.

"That's an interesting question, Neil." I held his eye in the mirror. Did he know about my parents? Had he used his cop resources to snoop around on me? "Why do you ask?"

"I think you'd find it refreshing."

"You know, my dad loved it out there."

"*He* did."

I nodded. He nodded with me.

"You can buy a mansion out there, right on the Bay of Fundy, for peanuts. You like seafood?"

"Mmhmm."

"The lobster walk right out of the Bay of Fundy and jump into your pot. You can get the best cup of chowder of your life at the gas station. You should check it out."

"Mm," I said. "Might do."

✂

Every night, my untroubled sleep drifted and swirled with men: their eyebrows, their voices, the veins in their hands, their grips, their gaits, their nose whistles, earlobes, the whites of their eyes … They gave me unselfish access, free from the usual masculine policing, and told me everything: their fears, their shames and frustrations. They let me share mine. It was intimate. I juggled a sense of loss as one man walked out the door with the excitement of watching the next one walk in, looking forward to the space he'd take up in my chair. When I was out in the world (or "their little cage," as Constance called it), waiting to cross the street, standing in line at the bank, ordering a sandwich, wherever, I'd find a man, move in closer, close my eyes, and think, *We are the same; let me hold some of what you're carrying*.

I wished my dad could have lived to see that not only had I not been conquered by the system, I'd infiltrated it and found kinship there. Constance praised my dedication to the "allegiance model": "We are united in the struggle and only together can we thrive. We cannot do it alone."

She often schooled me like this, entrusting me with her wisdom as though for safekeeping. It was strange; she had no compunction about favouring me outright over the other girls. You'd think it might have made things uncomfortable, but it didn't. I figured it must have had something to do with my dead parents. Every week, she asked me to groom her fuzzy sideburns with the clippers and trim her magnificent geometric fringe, which never seemed to turn grey. She could have done her own hair, of course, but whatever her reason for asking me instead, it was my favourite part of the week—largely for the five or six minutes she and I spent locked in the hot pod of noise created by the hair dryer as I pulled her bangs into their gentle curve between brush and air.

Just once, after I had just clicked off the switch, she asked, "Ever think what you'll do after this, Pup?"

"How do you mean?"

"You know, when you retire. Do you ever think about settling down? Loving someone?"

Suddenly defensive, I sputtered, "I do. Every day. I love—"

"Right, right." She nodded. "But you never wanted ... someone of your own?"

"*This* is what I want."

She studied my reflection. "Ever think about what you'll do when you're an old lady?"

"Well ... I hear you can buy a mansion for a dollar out on the East Coast. I could rock a cable-knit sweater and some hip waders, haunt the shore, scare the children ..."

"Ever think about them?"

"What, kids?"

"Mm."

I pulled the comb down her bangs, noticing one hair just slightly longer than the rest. Falcon eyed, I picked up my scissors and trimmed the strand. "It's never come up."

2009

MY APPOINTMENT WITH GORD WAS a Wednesday in September. I noticed it in the book as soon as it appeared. Sabrina and Tori were at the buffet, making espresso.

"Do you guys know Gordon?"

"Gordon …" said Sabrina. "Tor? Gordon?"

"Mmmm," said Tori, eyes on the ceiling. "Oh, Gord?"

"Says Gordon here."

"Yeah, I've had him. That's how he books. He's a good guy."

Gord was a four thirty. I was standing behind the reception desk when he arrived, and my fleeting thought as the door swung closed behind him was that his expensive fall overcoat was the same colour as the sky outside, which made it look like his head was floating. When the rest of him came into focus and I realized who he was, I nearly choked.

Mitch.

As Tori collected his overcoat, I somehow moved myself out from behind the desk.

"Louise, this is Gord."

I hadn't seen him since he graduated, which was, what, fifteen years ago? We hadn't spoken again after he'd snickered about my hair in the doorway of Physics class. I was thirty-one, which meant he was around thirty-three, rich and clean: grey suit, sky-blue tailored shirt, no tie, big pewter wedding band. He looked great. He looked successful. He also looked noticeably drawn, with puffed eyes. He was probably a work-hard-play-hard, fourteen-hour-day, chasing-every-buck office warrior, with sleep a small price to pay for the luxury he enjoyed. My anger flared. I'd hadn't thought of him much in all those years, but seeing him in person sent my bubbles rising.

I stared too long before greeting him in a rushed imitation of myself, unsure whether to acknowledge that I knew who he was. But his face clouded when he reached out his hand to me. The eyes searching mine weren't the hard little bullets seared into my memory but tired, sad pools of recognition. Shaking his hand was surreal, not just for the act of touching him, but also because his grip was warm and gentle. I pulled away.

"So … you two know each other," said Tori.

He nodded. I grappled, wide-eyed, with what to say, and somehow managed, "Can I get you a drink?"

"Yeah, maybe just a sparkling water. I'm picking up my daughter after this."

Daughter. Serves you right.

I cracked open a Perrier and perched lemon and lime wedges on the rim of his glass. When I handed it to him, he held my gaze, lips pursed, and gave me a sombre half nod.

"How *is* little Grace?" asked Tori, touching the back of his jacket as she led him to the booths.

Watching them disappear down the hall, a jittery thrill tickled my throat. I knew I wouldn't hurt him. Not at my place of work—I'm not an animal. But I'd also just seen the naked sincerity in his eyes. Not that I hadn't fallen for it before. Why was he even here? Tori had said he was fine. He didn't strike me as a bell ringer. How was he a "good guy"? I poured myself a flute of champagne, and my fingers throbbed against the crystal. I had him to myself for forty-five minutes. Forty-five. I'd never felt so electric.

Tori returned, serious. "What did he do to you?" she asked, pouring her own glass of champagne.

I exhaled and shook my head. "I can't describe it. It's so humiliating …"

"Do you want to swap? I've got Vlad."

"No." I gazed down the hallway. "I want him."

We ate a few handfuls of blueberries in silence. When I felt ready, I gulped down the last of my champagne, swished it through my teeth, and squeezed her hand.

No lamb is so precious …

I paused outside the door to my booth, my fist raised to knock, heart ragged despite my best attempts to rein it in. No matter how slowly I breathed, I couldn't convince my body that it wasn't about to fight. I shook my fingers. Constance was right across the hall. I didn't have to wonder what she'd do in my place. She'd give him the haircut of a lifetime, then find a moment to say, "You wronged me when we were children. I love and forgive us both, and I don't blame either of us for the world we were born into. Together, we'll do better." I channelled her with all my strength and knocked.

"Yup."

The fifty was folded politely under the bell, his jacket was hanging from the hook, and he sat in the shampoo chair, preoccupied.

The air took on a jelly-like consistency as I crossed the room, seething. I grappled with the sheer length of physical contact I'd need to have with him and concluded that for the forty-five minutes, while I ministered to his attractiveness, I would pretend my hands were controlled elsewhere, like the space arm. I relinquished tactile awareness.

"Well," he said. "I, uh, never would have guessed I'd find you working here."

"No? Why's that?" I reached for a towel, playing dumb.

He gestured vaguely at the ceiling. "It's just ... a pretty big coincidence." He pressed his fingers to his temples. "It's a really big coincidence."

"Mmhmm."

"Uh. You look good."

I laughed joylessly, but my self-esteem took note.

"Louise. That's your name, right?"

"That's right, *Gord*."

"Yeah, that's …" he weakly admitted, then returned to my name. "*Louise*. I don't know if I ever knew that."

Vaulting the threshold to contact, I ruffled his hair with my alien fingers. It was stiff with gel and I pulled it as I crunched a handful. "So what do you want done with this?"

"Ow, just a trim."

"Shave?"

"Not today."

I examined his sides and top and recommended an inch and a half, scissors, clippers just around the edges. Keep the top a little longer, point cut. "Hair as straight as yours needs a little variety at the ends."

"All right," he said.

"Enjoy it while you can. Those follicles won't last long. You're going to lose it all."

"Thanks."

"Yep."

Technically, he could have walked out. I both wondered and didn't care why he didn't. I wrapped the towel around his shoulders and lowered him into the neck rest, his throat tauntingly displayed. I imagined slicing it open and popping out his Adam's apple like a little apricot, but it was less enticing with it casually exposed.

He closed his eyes as the water coursed over his scalp; his brow was slightly knitted, and his eyes flickered under baby-bird lids. It felt unnatural, how easily he relinquished control. I lathered up my hands and waved them past his nose to see if he'd resist smelling the shampoo for fear of appearing feminine, but he flared his nostrils. I got the feeling he liked clean things. He was pliable for the rest of the wash and conditioning; we were both lost in thought. I brought him to the chair and draped him, and we looked at each other squarely in the mirror before he poked the indexes of his tented fingers out the front of the cape. "So, I'd like to apologize," he said.

I paused halfway to the Barbicide.

"It's hard for me to express to you how shitty I feel. About what we did to you. What *I* did to you."

The words danced in the air like colours I could touch.

"Honestly, I can't make it right, I can't make it go away, but I can apologize. It was a cruel and horrible thing to do. So horrible. And I'm sorry."

I barked a laugh, completely outside myself, and before I knew it my eyes had filled up. I turned so he wouldn't see my face in the mirror.

"I don't expect you to forgive me. I wouldn't if I were you, but I'm not a woman. I just want you to know that *I* know what I did was wrong, and that you've had to live with it all this time in a way I can never fully understand. But I am trying."

"Stop," I said. "Please." I crossed my arms. Behind me, I heard him stand. I raised a hand to stave him off.

"I know—it's not right of me to lay this on you here either," he said. "I'm, uh … well, I just wasn't expecting to see you."

I pushed my fists into my eyes until I saw red globs, then I stared at the red globs until I numbed back down.

"Okay, come on," I said.

He sat down and I spun him to face the mirror, then tapped a comb from the jar, parting his hair to reveal an ice-white, freckled scalp. The apology somehow made it harder to be nice. Having gone all this time with no retribution whatsoever, and then as soon as he shows up and I can take a crack at him, he cuts off my need to—I resented the decency, or its timing, at least.

"Well, I appreciate you saying all that, and you're right, it doesn't fix anything. But I'll bet *you* feel better, don't you?"

He nodded. "That's true."

I horseshoe-sectioned his hair and started scissor-over-combing on the right.

"I have a daughter now," he said.

"Aha."

"Well … it changes things."

I tilted his head forward. "That's such an old one. You spend your life disrespecting women and suddenly have a change of heart just because you have the bad luck to spawn a girl. Well, fuck you. Now you get to send her out into the world you assholes made."

"Grace," he said after a moment. "That's her name.

I know it doesn't matter, but she's smart and strong. I made sure of it."

"I'm sure you did. You know what kind of monsters lurk out there."

He looked into his lap.

"Well, I can't really disagree with that strategy, parenting-wise," I said.

"It would kill me to see her go through what I'm sure you went through."

"Well." I shook my head. "Do better. Toughening up one girl does nothing to fix the problem. She's not the one who needs changing. You understand that, right?"

"Yes."

"So start with respecting a woman who's not your own child. Protecting your own daughter doesn't make you a hero."

He nodded. I kept cutting.

"Stop moving. Why is that so hard?"

"What so hard?"

"Respecting women."

He paused for a moment before a long exhale. "I don't know," he said quietly, chastened. I almost felt I should ease off, but my adrenalin was up and I seemed to be winning.

"So does old Uncle Spence come over and bounce Grace on his knee?"

He gave me a warning look in the mirror.

"I mean, how close do you really let him get? Do you leave him alone with her?"

Mitch dropped his head between his shoulders and exhaled. "He, uh … he's …" He sucked in air. "He just … passed."

"…"

"On the weekend."

"Oh."

He quickly brought his fist to his mouth, nodding toward his hair. "I need the haircut for the—eulogy."

"Oh shit." I pulled my hands away. He gave me a desperate look of embarrassment as the last of his composure slipped. He crumpled in tears. I pocketed my scissors and stepped back. He lurched forward in the chair and grabbed his head with both hands.

"Agad." He shook with one big sob.

I approached him cautiously, like animal control. "Hey," I said, sending him into another juddering wave. "Hey …"

"It was such a stupid accident," he bawled. "I should have stopped him …"

One of the reasons Constance says men need to be better acquainted with their feelings is so that when this happens, it doesn't have to shatter the earth's very core. They're just tears. You're just sad. Let it bend you so you don't break.

"It's okay," I said, laying a hand on his back. He flung his head from side to side and I laid my other hand on his other shoulder. "It's okay." As the words left my mouth, his sobbing redoubled. He straightened and reached for me, the cape lifting around his neck and chin. Instinct compelled me backward, but my professional pride was stronger, and so I wrapped my arms around him, staring blank-eyed at myself in the mirror and straining against my heart's breach. Not for him. Not for him ...

"I'm sorry," he moaned. "I'm going to miss him so bad."

"I know." My anger thrashed against my desire to comfort him, in a riotous match, but the tilt was already underway, and the warmth rushed down from the top of my head.

"I'm sorry we did that to you. I'm so sorry."

I rested my head against his head, surrendering completely. "I know," I said softly. "I forgive you."

><

When I was eight, Barry dismembered my Pulsar: Ultimate Man of Adventure doll while our moms were upstairs. My Pulsar and Barry's G.I. Joe were robbing a bank. Pulsar was supposed to wait in the getaway car while G.I. Joe went into the bank, but since G.I. Joe was taking his sweet time inside, playing a little cat and mouse with the tellers, Pulsar got a head start on building the lean-to in Hawaii where they'd flee once they'd escaped with the money, using the couch cushions and stereo cabinet. When G.I. Joe came running out of the bank and Pulsar wasn't in the car, Barry got upset. G.I. Joe could have driven the car himself, but Barry didn't like to be ignored. He wasn't a mean kid, but I guess he was worked up from the thrill of the robbery. He grabbed Pulsar and started dancing him around in the air. I watched, frozen solid, as the dance got sexier and Barry pulled off one of Pulsar's arms. Then the other. Then his legs. Then he popped off Pulsar's head and—like the climax of a striptease—pressed the button on his back to activate the heart and lungs of his headless torso. I remember the signal whine in my ears as I broke with the moment in our wood-panelled basement. I imagined twisting Barry's right arm tighter and tighter until the flesh split, the tendons snapped, and his humerus popped right out the top of his shoulder.

He ended up telling on himself upstairs, and his mother made him apologize and promise to buy me a new Pulsar with his allowance. But after that, any time I looked at him, all I saw was that dance, and the look on his face, and the *flavour* of harm he knew he was doing. A new Pulsar didn't erase that.

I asked my dad about it while he was beating me at cribbage that night.

"Dad, should I punch Barry in the face?"

"Why?"

"Because of what he did to Pulsar. Will it make me feel better?"

He laid his cards on my bedspread. "Lou," he said, "Barry is a good kid who did a stupid thing. Forgiving stupidity is easy, and I'd almost suggest you do it here just for the practice. But real forgiveness, where the bad thing melts away and you can look at the person who did it and not even see it anymore, where you can maybe even love them, is like nothing else on earth. Forgiveness feels so … *euphoric*. It's always worth considering. Grudges are heavy." He lifted his cards. "But if you're going to hold one, make it a good one. And stick to it. Now look at this hand!"

He was right: forgiving was euphoric. Not that I'd spent every night fixating on Mitch, but releasing the malice I'd carried lifted such a weight from my mind and heart. The ability to think of him as a good man elevated me to another plane. I mean, this was considered divine.

And that apology! He'd claimed responsibility, he'd expressed regret, he'd promised to do better ... He'd even given me the option not to accept, after admitting that he himself would not have. It was a masterpiece. Forgiving Mitch made me feel wise and kind; I was a better me, moving into my next phase of maturity. I'd gotten my wings. When I couldn't sleep at night, I'd replay that appointment in my mind, not just as a reminder that remorse could be felt by someone so foul, but as a reminder to myself of how worthwhile it is to be gentle. And then I would sleep deeply and happy, secure in the goodness of the world and my part in it.

✂

I was floating from one of those sleeps when, a few weeks after Mitch's appointment, I awoke to a biblical rain. My underground garage door opened to reveal a waterfall. It felt so unnatural that for the first time in my years working at Hair for Men I thought of taking a sick day. But I had a book full of appointments, and if anything would put things right, it was my clients.

At a red light halfway to work, I was turning up the volume on Nick Cave—his voice was too low to hear over my wipers—when a woman crossed in front of my car. She could have been thirty or sixty, and she wore a pair of orange Crocs, a grey raincoat, and little else. Tendons protruded behind her knees like wires. It was pouring rain with twenty-kilometre-per-hour winds, and her legs were bare. Something frilly poked out the bottom of her raincoat, like half a skirt, or the lining of the coat, maybe a slip. She was crossing very slowly. As she passed my windshield, I got a better look at the coat's grey pattern: it was a series of overlapped black-and-white images that, on closer inspection, arranged themselves into porn. My eyes worked to adjust. The raincoat was made of a waterproof fabric printed with pornographic images—spread legs, cupped tits. As she neared the opposite curb, I got a look at her back, where, printed in the correct Larry Flynt magazine font, was the word HUSTLER. Lower down, among the overlapped images, was the word BEST. She shuffled up onto the sidewalk, pulled a free newspaper from the box, and held it pointlessly over her head. How did a coat like that even get made, and how had it found its way onto this woman? Had she won it? What would normally qualify as a regular urban sight today felt like a sign.

When I arrived, the phone was ringing. "Hair for Men," I said, pulling back my hood.

"Yeah, hi," a man's voice answered.

"Hi," I said, and waited. "Are you looking to make an appointment?"

"Well now, what comes with that appointment?" A laugh. We got these calls occasionally, but today, like everything else, it felt different.

"Sir, we're a hair salon." I cradled the phone under my chin as I opened the green book. "Revolutionary cut, shave, and style."

The line went dead.

I held the receiver to my chest and leaned back to look down the hall. "Hello?" I called out like the first girl to die in the movie. No answer. I turned on the espresso maker and set up the bar in the unnerving quiet.

The front door opened, amplifying the rain for a second as Sabrina walked in, shaking off her cherry-red raincoat.

"What is going *on*?" she said, tilting her head toward the door. "That rain's not natural. Is it?"

"No, it's not," I said. "And we just got another one of those calls."

She gave me an ominous look as she came to stand next to me at the mimosa station. I made two and we toasted somewhat ceremoniously. She held my gaze as we drank.

At eleven forty-five, right before lunch, I was just starting to shave the left side of Angelo's face when I heard a commotion in the hall. Our eyes met in the mirror. Angelo gripped the armrests as the door burst open. Bulletproof-vested officers shouldered in with frenzied shouting, pointing guns. We raised our hands, and two officers cuffed Angelo and whisked him away, half his face still lathered. Another officer shook the razor from my hand. He grabbed my coat from the closet and threw it at me.

"Put that on." Once I had, he cuffed me too.

Out in the hall, there must have been twenty more cops. I made out the top of Sabrina's golden head close to the front door. When our eyes met, hers implored me in a way I couldn't discern. In the melee, I glimpsed the jerky, swishing ponytail of Bree, our intern. And then the officer started to drag me by an arm toward the front doors. I searched for Constance, craning my head up to see above everyone, and spotted her being escorted from her office.

"Constance!" I yelled over the officer's shoulder.

"You don't want to do that." He hustled me along.

Out in the lot, I saw Augustus was handcuffed; his soaked T-shirt looked like it had melted into his skin. An officer stood on either side of him, holding him by a bicep—they hadn't even let him get his coat. My officer directed me to the open door of one of the flashing cruisers. I jumped up and gave a last look back for Constance just as the officer pushed my head down like they do on TV, sending my eye into the door frame. I hadn't been hit in the face in years, and I bellowed with the old vitality. The door slammed shut.

"What are you doing?" The cop in the front seat shouted through the driver's side window.

"I'm sorry, she moved."

The windshield wipers were on full, clearing momentary patches in the endless rain. The cruiser was dark, the engine's drone almost soothing. Blood trickled down my eyelid. "This is fucking police brutality, you know," I said, kicking the partition. "What's going on??"

"Hey!" barked the cop in the front seat through the grate. He was in full uniform, hat and everything.

"Neil! What the fuck?"

"It's Officer Osborne," he said. "You need to know you're not under arrest, but I swear to god, if you test me, I will not hesitate to throw you right in with the rest of your friends."

"Are you serious? Is this ... are you busting us??"

He put the car in gear and pulled out of the lot.

"Where are we going? What's going to happen to them?"

"We're shutting you down for solicitation. Your new girl, Bree, is a negotiator. I wish she'd made it harder for us."

I was speechless.

✄

Bree was from California, studying at the Christof Gallant Institute in Los Angeles. She had an aunt in Toronto and had written Constance to ask if she could intern with us to make up the salon hours for her licence. Tori had just gotten an opportunity to tour with the Berlin Philharmonic for two months, so her booth was free. Bree had put together a portfolio of her styling shots and colour accomplishments. She'd included a headshot of herself wearing a tall blue ponytail like Nina Hagen—or a My Little Pony—and a torn wedding dress, lipstick smeared across her face. Constance decided she looked like fun, and we agreed, pleased at the chance to help a young stylist.

We were a little taken aback when Bree showed up for her first shift. She had tiny features like Tinkerbell, and her ponytail was an immaculate cotton-candy pink, but she was dressed in a Juicy Couture track suit, a choice that was awfully ... popular. Sabrina and I exchanged a look, but Constance made it clear that she would never question a woman's aesthetic choice, and we didn't question Constance. We figured it was a California thing.

"So men only, eh?" Bree asked as I showed her how to load the hot-towel machine on her first day. She had a voice that made things sound sleazy.

I laughed. "I thought the same thing, but no. It's different."

"Ugh," she said, crinkling her nose.

"No," I said, very serious. "This is different."

Her "Oh-kay" had me worry I'd overemphasized, or incorrectly emphasized, so I whispered to her the same thing that had been said to me: "You're going to love it."

Watching her set off down the hall for her first appointment with her little fists clenched, I resisted the urge to stop her and tell her what she was in for. She emerged from that appointment with a furtive look, like she'd proved something.

✂

"Fetish services, Louise," said Neil. "You know what went on."

I opened my mouth and the air was sucked clear out of my lungs.

"Oh, you think no one's getting hurt, but the rot creeps in slowly. You think, what's a few men? What harm can it do? Well, I'll explain something to you: the world is able to function day by day because certain structures are in place based on competence and reason, and those structures keep us all safe—you included. You start weakening those structures, and you open the gates to chaos. I'm not going to stand by and watch that happen."

"Fetish services," I repeated, staggered, "I can't ..."

"Pretty sick stuff," he said.

"Are we talking about the same thing?"

"Trust me, I'm doing this for you too."

It was like he was speaking English backward. He didn't seem to be a part of reality.

"Where will you go to talk about Crowded House? And your garden?"

He gave me a look in the rear-view mirror. "That stuff's made up, Louise. It's a persona I use for undercover work."

I shook my head. "No, it's not. It's you. You run outside first thing in the morning to check for fresh sprouts. The sight of a newborn pansy bud makes you weep for the fragility of life. You can't fool me—you said those things. You need it as bad as the rest of them!"

"I don't need anything, least of all to explain myself to you. Now, I'm taking you home. I suggest you pack some things and make yourself scarce for a while. I've called in a favour on your behalf."

"Why?"

He shrugged. "Why don't *you* count your blessings?"

I fumed out the window, grudgingly beholden to him as it sank in how much worse this could be.

"Look, you're a smart girl," he said into the mirror. "You don't want to deal with charges, hire a lawyer, go through the courts … Trust me. Let your friends figure this out for themselves. But they're eventually going to find out you're not under arrest, which makes you look like a rat. Running an establishment like this isn't a high felony or anything, so if they get any jail time, it won't be much. They'll notice you're not with them once they get downtown."

The horizon darkened around the cruiser, the rest of the ride along the 401 miserable and grey. Toronto had never looked as brutally ugly as it did right then.

He pulled over a few streets from mine to let me out and uncuff me so my whole condo building didn't have to watch.

"How am I supposed to get my car?"

"You'll have to go back later. There won't be a guard."

"When?"

"Shouldn't be long. Wait for dusk."

"Dusk … you're a fucking poet."

"I'm going to miss our visits, Louise."

"I *know* you are!"

He shook his head like I'd forced him to say it. "Did you know you were the only one there using your real name?"

The revelation seeped in, coating my heart like lead. The sense of inclusion that had defined my work life dissolved as the weight took hold, revealing me, completely alone. I'd been orphaned all over again, and the quickest relief I could find, paired with the desire to spit in the face of authority— as though this was Officer Osborne's fault for having told me—was to twist my face into a hideous mask and glare furiously at him as I rammed my fist over and over into my split eyebrow. The bleeding started fresh, and I tried to focus my anger, but my knees buckled and I dropped to the sidewalk. Neil got out of the cruiser and flipped up his collar. As he approached, I turtled my back against him and covered my head with my hands. Blood dripped from my eyebrow into a puddle of rainwater as he knelt beside me.

I wrenched away from him and wrapped myself up tighter, the rain pelting my coat.

"Look, I'm sorry, but you need to think about the future. You're going to have a life after this. Go out east. You said yourself it looks like a nice place to live—cheap, friendly, good seafood … Just go and cut regular hair."

I pushed myself up onto all fours. "I DON'T WANT TO CUT REGULAR HAIR!"

From there, I could have easily tackled him, wrestled him

down, and grabbed his gun. I could have jumped in the cruiser and held up the police station until they let everyone go, then we could all have run away together to Hawaii and started a new Hair for Men. I might have actually considered it, if not for the physical sickness I felt at finding myself on the outside of a place where I'd felt so sure I belonged.

Officer Osborne stood up and reached for my hand. I smacked his hand away. He held it out again. "You have to get up."

I stared at the rubber soles of his cop boots. They were much more like sneakers in real life.

"Louise."

His fingers filled my view, raindrops pooling in the creases of his palm.

"So is Neil *your* real name?" I asked bitterly from under the shell of my body.

"No," he said. "It's Tim."

✂

Once home, I paced the floor, working out my strategy. It was ridiculous to think anyone was coming after me, but for the sake of a little distance until things blew over, I would take Officer Osborne's advice and get out of town. I packed a bag, purgatorially watching the CP24 newsfeed, killing time until it was dark. My eye puffed up as the day wore on, but I refused the relief of icing it. The pain was a happy distraction. Picking up the car gave me a task and a timeline, while the TV cushioned me from thoughts other than each moment as it arrived, keeping my mind clear of past and future. I watched the reports on the storm, the flooding, the resulting backups on the 401, and more, as I planned my escape route. The announcers' voices blended into a sort of mush, like the commentary on an unfamiliar sport, until just after six, when, loud and clear, the lady announcer said, "Also this hour, arrests at a Mississauga hair salon."

I hovered in front of the TV as they showed an ad for the guy who buys your used gold for cash. After a fade to black, a trenchcoated reporter appeared, standing *in front of my car.* Police tape circled the parking lot behind her.

"Peel Police have made several arrests," she intoned with matter-of-fact disbelief, "at this Mississauga hair salon—trading in fetish services—in a sting that's been underway for months.

I braced myself on the sofa as she continued.

"*This* local merchant says he had *no* idea it was *going on* right under their noses."

"They kept to themselves," said old Mr. Delorme, wearing his butcher's apron, "but you knew to see them, men coming and going all day long, something wasn't right."

I'd been waiting all those hours, I realized, hoping for proof there'd been a mistake and we could all go back to normal. But here was Hair for Men on TV, seemingly caught red-handed. What self-respecting barbershop was going to hire me now? Not that I could even think about cutting hair again. The passion that had once ignited me now felt freeze-dried in my veins, and for the very first time the thought crossed my mind: *It's a good thing your parents aren't alive.*

I settled back on my bed, waiting obsessively for more coverage. Stabbing at Jane and Finch, Intake Spikes at East End Shelter, Seniors Found Guilty in Caterer's Death. Not another word about us. In fact, the headline didn't make it twice through the loop, leaving me to doubt whether I'd seen it in the first place. Nothing felt solid. I consumed every line of the feed until seven thirty, at which point I assumed there couldn't reasonably be anyone left in Turcott Industrial Park, and I hit the elevator button.

Fetish services …

I covered my head with my hood and made my way through the lobby and into an orange-and-green Beck cab. The driver ferried me through the forest of factories, never once raising an eyebrow or glancing at me in the mirror. He laid his open palm beneath his ear to collect my fare.

As the cab's engine ebbed away, the sound of the street lights rose like cicadas. If Turcott Industrial Park was quiet at peak industry during the day, at night it was a tomb. The rain had stopped, but a fine mist lingered. Beneath the low-pressure sodium lights, the Passat gleamed through its dewy veil, the only car in the lot. There was no night patrol, and the caution tape had been removed. There was the front door, undamaged, waiting for me to walk through it and flip the switch for the chandelier. Instead, I stood on the sidewalk, clutching my fob and taking a good look around before hitting the Unlock button. The interior lit up, the only car for blocks, and the horn chirped tactlessly. I stepped over the grass partition and reached for the door handle. A whiff of cloves and carnation snatched my breath away.

"Hello, Pup."

She gasped when I turned. My eye was swollen shut by then, and I'd almost gotten used to looking through just the other one.

"Did they do that to you?" she asked with hushed disbelief, leaning in for a better look.

"Yes—no," I said, staring at her jeans and red windbreaker. She didn't seem to mind her frizzled hair, or seem at all angry that I wasn't in police custody.

I waited for an accusation, for my clean arrest record held up as proof of my disloyalty or insider advantage, but she looked relieved to see me.

"I didn't rat us out, you know."

"I know," she said with a sad laugh. "If there's anyone I'm sure of, it's you."

"Is that because I was the only one stupid enough to use my real name?"

She gazed up into the stars, then down at me. "No, Louise. It's because in all my time, I've never seen anyone with your ... well, your natural aptitude. You truly believed."

"Of course I did. It was my job!"

"No. It goes deeper with you. Your patience and, my

god, your optimism. I watched you over the years, and ...
well, you're different. I'll admit right here that even *I've*
never had your faith—not to mention that ... I don't know
if you've noticed, but I've been slipping myself. If it hadn't
been Bree, it would have been something else."

"Wait, they told you it was her?"

She nodded. "I wasn't as cautious with her as I should
have been. That's on me."

It was surreal speaking out loud about any of it. Imagine
if we'd been able to discuss this all along. Imagine if we'd all
been talking about the same thing.

"You've been *slipping?*" I emphasized to make sure I'd
heard right.

She sighed. "It wears you out. All that pretending. In a
way, it's true what the police are calling it. But it was an
escape, that's all. We were giving those men a place to hide,
because they have too much to lose and they're terrified.
They're not willing to risk it. At a certain point, we have
to cut our losses. When you consider how unlikely it is that
we're even alive on this planet, let alone that we made all
that money ..."

"So what are you doing here?"

"I knew you'd come back for your car. I considered not
coming, but ... I couldn't just let you go."

I held my breath, not sure what I was hoping for.

She contemplated me with a sort of wonder. "Don't be
discouraged. I know it seems ridiculous, but don't let this

snuff out your flame. I'm too old and too tired, but you …
You have a gift."

"It's not a very useful gift without my job," I muttered,
though deliriously flattered by her praise.

"You'll find a way. I know you will."

"What are you going to do?"

"I'm going away for a while—maybe a long while. I have
a friend in BC with a farm where I can lay low, which I'd
suggest you do too. Take this opportunity to go somewhere
you've always wanted to go. Leave tonight. You have the
money—do something for yourself."

I looked at my feet. "Say hey to Auggie for me."

"Ugh." She lifted a palm. "I'm going alone. I've had
enough of them."

"But …" How was she saying these things? "He's one of
the good ones."

"Oh, Louise …" she said, "there's no such thing."

As she walked away, I thought to ask her name, but
stopped myself. I didn't want to know.

I idled in the parking lot for a long time, waiting for the
impulse to pull away from the slab walls I worried had held
my best days. I stared stonily at the door and ran a mental
inventory of all the men who'd walked through it, imagining
their lights snuffed out like candles. I put on Diamanda Galás's
"The Sporting Life," a song in which she and some of her
friends rape Snoop Dogg, and shifted the car into gear. As
I drove out of the lot for the last time, I kept one eye on the

Mississauga sky above, where the constellations were extinguished, one star at a time.

✂

I drove through the night, seized every so often by waves of doubt, talking myself back through the events. I stopped three times at Tim Hortons for coffee but was too emotionally queasy to even consider one of their sensible ham and cheese sandwiches. By the time I reached Edmundston the next morning, my stomach was eating itself, so I pulled into a Big Stop for breakfast. At this hour, I would normally have been nibbling peach slices, rolling up the wet towels for the heater and spritzing them with frankincense.

When the woman at the truck stop counter walked over to pour my coffee, she got a look at my face and stopped halfway with the pot. I waved the air like it was a stupid misunderstanding; she cocked her head in tired resignation and poured. The truckers sitting farther down the counter peeked out from under their hat brims. Watching the news on the TV set above their heads, one of them reached out and tapped the arm of the one next to him. Each man took out a lottery ticket from his back pocket and alternated looks between the ticket and the TV.

"Win anything?" asked the first one.

"Naw," said the other. "Lost again."

My breakfast arrived to more rubbernecking from the

truckers. I had ordered everything: four eggs, a pancake, toast, hash browns, bacon, sausage, and a slab of fried bologna, which I poked with my fork and held up like a prize.

The trucker next to me leaned over. "You put ketchup on that."

I thanked him and squeezed a reservoir of ketchup onto my plate.

He leaned in closer. "I hope you gave him one right back."

"Oh," I said. "No, it's ..."

He nodded and winked. He would have been in his sixties, plaid shirt, work pants, hair growing out of the pores on his nose.

He directed a finger toward my bologna. "Me, I just dump 'er right on there."

The news told us about a diabetes fundraiser, a town hall to address potholes, and a stoplight being installed at the intersection near the mall entrance. The less familiar the news, the deeper it sank in what lay behind. I was somewhere else now. The land of fried bologna.

I booked myself into a Best Western near the highway and slept for a few hours before I started looking at Craigslist. I didn't know if I'd stay a week or a year, but I was unemployed, with an unexpectedly criminal past. I only had so many options. And then the unadorned utility of one ad caught my eye:

Boat + Job

I had nothing to keep me occupied, so the job wasn't a bad idea. Although I still had my scissors, I had no intention of cutting hair. If the headline of the ad was intriguing, it was the job title in the description that really sold me. Being a "Dockmaster" sounded great, and I could handle the "light cleaning." There were two photos attached to the posting: a blurry shot of some drunk people (possibly) fighting (?) around a fire, and the view out a window of the harbour at sunset. I stuffed down two lobster rolls at the next Big Stop on the way out of town, the whole while fixated on the view of that harbour as it appeared on my phone.

The Craigslist ad had included a phone number and address, which, for safety reasons, you're not supposed to do, so I had some sense of who I'd be dealing with. It was just before dusk when I showed up at Cradle Bay marina. After ringing the clubhouse's doorbell and getting no response, I walked around to the side of the building, where I could see a light in a window curtained by a Moosehead Lager beach towel. A man was singing along to Alanis Morissette's "You Learn." I knocked on the pane and the singing stopped. After some shuffling, a figure appeared. I waved, and he waved back, gesturing around to the front. I wondered whether he'd forgotten the appointment when he came shambling up to the door, the brim of his ball cap silhouetted against the hall light behind him. He looked almost put out by the interruption until he noticed my eye.

"Jeez," he said, and he pulled me inside, then checked behind me before closing the door. "You okay?"

Right then, I had a few choices. I hadn't considered the need for a backup story, nor had I anticipated the intensity of his concern, so I just nodded and said, "Yeah, thanks," hoarding the unearned sympathy.

Stealing occasional glances at my face, he showed me around the club. A permanently moored boat called The Pill served as living quarters for the job. After the tour, he reached a hand out to the boat's lifeline.

"Well, guess it's not much of a place for a lady."

"That's good," I said, "since I don't see any fucking ladies inquiring."

He threw his head back. "Ha! All right then." He shook my hand with his big, callused paw.

"This calls for a tall green one!" he said, leading me back up to the clubhouse. We climbed the stairs to the bar, where a golden sunset shimmered across the surface of the harbour through the bay window.

I'd learn that "*a* tall green one" was a drink, and "*The* Tall Green One" was the red Rubbermaid tumbler the Commodore used for his rum and Cokes. The story went that one night, after too many tall green ones, he'd fallen, hooting and splashing, off the diesel dock. After his wife, Jenny, had fished him out with the boathook, she'd drily asked, "Do you think you've had enough, Bruce?" In response, he'd gone to the clubhouse, cut the bottom out of the tumbler with his hunting knife, and put it up on the shelf over his desk so he'd never forget. Then he'd taken the red tumbler from the same Rubbermaid set and started using that. The original Tall Green One, which was green, still sat over his desk as an homage to Jenny, who had since moved on.

"C'mon up here," he said, leading me to the big oak table in front of the window. He poured us a rum and toasted me wordlessly. Then, with the index finger of the hand that held the tumbler, he pointed through the window. For close to an hour we watched in silence as the sun sank and lit the cove crimson. In that hour, my heart might have beaten four times. I needed nothing. I'd forgotten we didn't know each other until out of nowhere he said, "So, you like the Hip?" The question hit me like a shower of ice.

"Uhh ... never really got into them, no."

"Good Ontario girl like you doesn't like the Hip?" he said, already out of his chair. He crossed to the bar and turned on the stereo, doing a little dance as he returned with the bottle. "Ho, ho, ho, we'll see about that ..."

I stiffened. I was an adult, of course, not a rabbity teenager, but the sound of The Tragically Hip still sent me back into the woods behind the bleachers with a vividness I'd thought should have faded with the years. I may have forgiven, but I'd never—ever—forget.

"Back before I bought this place," said the Commodore, "I used to be a sound tech in Halifax. I've seen the Hip twenty-seven times. Gord Downie is probably one of the nicest people I ever met. One time when they were playing the Metro Center, I remember, their tour bus got a flat. It was pouring rain, and I was the guy who got to change the tire. While I was out there, Gord came out of the bus and stood with me, getting soaked, telling me about learning to change a tire when he was a kid. I remember him just wiping the rain off his face with his hand. He took the time to talk with me, about his childhood. In the rain." He shook his head and drifted off for a moment. "Here," he said, and he clapped his palms on his thighs. He stood up again and came back with a cribbage board and a deck of cards.

"You play?"

"… Yeah …" I said.

He shuffled. "Good. If I beat you, *Fully Completely* is just twelve songs. I think you've got it in you. Because I will," he said, placing the deck in front of me to cut, "beat you."

My heart went soft at the sound of his shit-talking. I cut a nine of hearts. "I so look forward," I said, "to never hearing this album."

He cut a jack of clubs and shuffled the player to another CD. "Meantime, do you like Alanis Morissette?"

Cribbage has such a simple set of rules that there are almost no regional differences. His counting cadence—fifteen two, fifteen four, fifteen six, three are nine—was the same as my dad's. We played an evenly matched game, but with the help in the final hand of some last-minute pegging and a run on his six and my four with his five, he thundered ahead to the finish.

"Ready?" He lifted the remote.

I'd been sedated by the comfort of crib and rum—we were finishing up our second—and had forgotten what we were even playing for. I somehow at that moment felt so content that I couldn't find the resistance.

"All right," I said. "Let's do it."

"Here we go." He hit Play. "Hope you like A minor."

At the first chords of "Courage" I felt a pressure in my chest, but I listened stoically. The Commodore closed his eyes and dipped his head, swaying bearlike to and fro, listening with full intensity. He clearly loved this song, which for some reason made me want to love it too. I couldn't make sense of the lyrics, but I was feeling okay with the melody, and even with the sound of Gord Downie's voice, which had always struck me as *mocking*. Like he was in cahoots with my unbothered tormentors—not maliciously, but idly, like a cat.

As he handed me the deck to deal the next game, the Commodore said, "It's the ultimate act of subversion, Louise. They're this mainstream, white guy bar band, and the Great Man—Gord—writes sensitive lyrics that go miles over the heads of his main audience. He can make a room full of frat boys recite poetry. He can make them sing from *The Watch That Ends the Night*—and they don't have a clue. 'There is no simple explanation for anything important any of us do, and the human tragedy, or the human irony, consists in the necessity of living with the consequences of actions performed under the pressure of compulsions so obscure we do not and cannot understand them.' That's Hugh MacLennan. That's

Canadian literature. That's what Gord just sang." The Commodore threw his head back. "Hah!"

There was a time I'd have been the first one to loudly tell you that The Tragically Hip were mainstream bullshit. But the Great Man had tricked the hockey goons with poetry. He'd fooled them into believing he wasn't giving them high art. *Devil* … Listening to The Tragically Hip with the Commodore was like deciphering a foreign language. It felt like a gift.

When "Locked in the Trunk of a Car" came on, he told me, "This one's great. It's about a guy driving around with a body in the trunk of a car. No one really knows, but it might be about the October Crisis there in Quebec, where they ended up killing that guy they kidnapped. Though I've always thought it might just be about carrying something around you want to get rid of. Like a feeling, or a memory." He had a real way of bringing me around to his side, and when Gord Downie screamed "Let me out!" at the end, I honestly thought, *This is a good song*.

At one point, the Commodore turned and took a long look at my black eye, his face clouded with the violence he wanted me to know he'd be willing to commit against the man he believed had blackened it. That he was a good enough man to want to hurt someone he'd never met. "By the way," he said, "you don't have to worry. You'll be safe here."

Nothing was stopping me from putting him straight, except that I'd already decided the straight story wouldn't be making the rounds. It's amazing that something as splendid as Hair for Men could have been so debauched by exposure to light. But yeah, from the outside, it looked bad.

I decided my only crime here would be to let the Commodore believe I'd fled one man, not hundreds.

2016

I JOLT AWAKE AND STRETCH my eyes wide open. The dream was so bright and clear that I have to check my mental inventory from yesterday to make sure I haven't actually killed someone, because for all that I'm lying in my berth aboard The Pill with no duffle bag of remains, there's something in the air, just a hint, that smells like the dream is still going on. I focus on the letters *King Cole Tea* on the towel stuffed into the edges of the hatch overhead. I pass my hand over the woollen upholstery of the forward berth cushion and grab the blue nylon of my sleeping bag, holding it in front of my eyes. These things are real. But when I inhale deeply, I'm struck by the faint but unmistakable stench of an inlet filled with rotting men. I rummage around in my sleeping bag for my Bad Brains T-shirt. Then my hoodie. I slide out of my bunk and poke my head out the companionway hatch.

In the cockpit, the morning fog hangs heavy. The stink is more powerful out here and I slap my face twice to make sure I'm awake. The yard is silent, so I can't tell if I'm the only one experiencing the smell. I poke my nose down the neck of my T-shirt. It's not me. I smell like a mechanic's rag, but I smell like me.

Today is a big day—both here at the marina and for the rest of Canada. Gord Downie was diagnosed with brain cancer back in May, and tonight is the Hip's final show in Kingston. We're airing the CBC broadcast in the clubhouse tonight, and all the members are coming. It'll be a big, sad party.

The Commodore, it goes without saying, has been … struggling. He's been flailing between the stages of the grief cycle but has spent most of his time in anger and bargaining, expounding on the unfairness of it all because Downie is so loved and so needed. When we listen to the Hip now, you can see it in his face, the way he broods out at the harbour; he's negotiating with an unseen force for the return of Gord Downie's health.

In addition to the show, a vessel on its way down the coast is coming in from Toronto to rent a berth for the night. When you're travelling through Saint John on the Down East Circle Route along the Atlantic Coast, you need to go through the Reversing Falls, a deceptively named series of rapids that'll run you aground if you venture through at the wrong tide. It's a menace, and not just a disappointment for the tourists who come looking for the upside down waterfall. Our marina is conveniently located in a protected cove where boats can wait for slack tide to get safely through the Falls. The Commodore says the boat is on its way to Cape Breton, which still gives me a jolt.

Back in the cabin, I wash up and braid my hair, all grown out from my tophawk days. Most is still gingery, some a woolly grey. There's a proper shower in the clubhouse where I keep a set of flip-flops and a towel, but I don't go dragging myself up there first thing. Or even daily.

In the galley, I open the Tupperware bin that protects my work pants from the morning condensation. These pants are not so much clothing as a storage unit. Like the trunk of a car. Every night before bed, I take out my Leatherman and lay it on the galley table like an offering. It's got straight, serrated, wood, and metal saws, coarse and fine files, needle-nose pliers with wire cutters and strippers, and a screwdriver fitting. Along with the key ring that drags down my waistband, these are the tools of my trade now. That ring contains keys to locks I haven't seen in years. For the sake of my belt loops I should get rid of half of them, but I've grown sentimental.

I still have a pair of my Mizutanis—tucked in my smock pocket when the police busted in—but I only take them out of their protective sheath from time to time to snip the ends of my own hair. I miss their sweet, crisp sound.

The waves slurp against the hull as I stretch my face to the sky. Aside from the stench of meat, it's a perfect day. Once the fog burns off around noon, it'll be sunny straight on through. August on the Fundy Coast is no July, but it's nice enough. It's also Saturday, not that that matters much, but it does add a little something. Weekends only apply to the working folks who moor their boats here so they can make use of their marina fees for competitive, overnight cockpit drinking with the luxury of collapsing in their own berth and no drive home.

Turns out I'm well suited to dockmastering, though the job's really just like a gas attendant and groundskeeper for boats. Sure, I have to pick up beer cans on the shore, but I fall asleep at night to the sound of the waves, and my time is my own. Mornings I get up, make the big canteen of coffee before the Commodore's awake, tend to anyone needing diesel, then roam the grounds making small repairs and restocking empty things—"mastering the docks," as we say—until lunch. After that I'll read in the "hut"—the closet-sized wooden shed next to the gas pumps—where I watch for incoming vessels looking to gas up or buy ice, until it's time for my nap. When I wake up, the Commodore is usually on his first (or so) green one, and if the members are around there'll be a bonfire blazing on the concrete slab between the docks. If not, the Commodore and I will play cribbage up in the clubhouse until I drift off to The Pill and he goes down to sleep in his office.

In the hut, I read books about the sea. My fluffy, amber-paged copy of Bernard Moitessier's *The Long Way* is currently sitting there on the painted shelf beneath my lookout window. Moitessier sailed around the world in the Golden Globe race in 1968 along with the ill-fated Donald Crowhurst. After Crowhurst had fallen off the map, once every other competitor had been conquered by the mission and Moitessier was in the home stretch with Robert Knox-Johnson, Moitessier decided to head back out for another spin. Around the planet. He saw his family standing there on the pier, the wife and kids he hadn't seen in the year since he'd set out in the competition, and he just switched tack and left them there, waving. Life on land had become inconceivable. Soldiers returning from combat go through a similar dissociation from the civilization they knew before they lived its opposite. For Moitessier, there was no life without the sea. It's a feeling I've come to understand.

The Commodore taught me to sail as soon as I got here, determined not to have a landlubber on staff. He took me out every day in the Flying Juniors to learn the basics. From there, I used my instincts, acquiring a sense for finding the wind and putting it in my sails. I hadn't realized how addictive it could be. I envy smokers their ability to just get up and walk out of social engagements in order to fulfill a generally accepted need; you can't sneak out for a quick sail.

I set off toward the clubhouse, performing a little low-grade maintenance as I go—coiling some loose lines, pulling the bow of The Elephant Man around on the shore so it's in line with the rest of the Juniors. When I look up, the Commodore is shuffling down the gravel toward me in his Tevas, holding a grape Popsicle in one hand and my coffee mug in the other.

I stop. He got up before me, and he's made the coffee. He raises the Popsicle to his eyes and hands me my mug.

"Hell's that smell, Lou?"

Because of his old-school chivalry, the Commodore took some time to get past my gender. But I was patient, I put in the work, and look at us now: the man treats me like a brother-in-law.

"Wait, this is for me?"

"Why's that so hard to believe?"

"Well, thank you." I take a sip and it's fine.

"See? There. You're welcome." He slurps the Popsicle. "All you gotta say. I've had four cups, myself. Now I got the sweats." He lifts the arm with the hand holding the Popsicle and fans his armpit. He only ever wears plaid shirts with the sleeves cut off. His armpits are a constant in my life.

"Guy, that's too much coffee." I've never called him Commodore, because it implies my occupying a rank beneath him, and "Bruce" is too intimate.

He puts his hand over his heart. "Naw, it's fine."

"Why are you even up?"

"I been working on something. I'll show you later."

He seems in good spirits, but I go gently. "How ... are you doing?"

"How d'you mean?"

"About tonight."

He winces into the horizon, gathering his thoughts, then looks at me.

"We're all going to die, Louise. The best we can do is fill a shockingly small number of waking hours with something we enjoy, with the people we like most. That's what I'm going to try and do. No more."

"Okay."

"I have to stop thinking how unfair it is, how young he is … Life is random and cruel, and look at all we've got." He gestures with his Popsicle toward the fog. "Look at this day!"

It feels like he's arrived at the acceptance stage today, but I can't be sure he's taking the steps in order. Nonetheless, his mood is better.

We stand a moment, appraising the snug opacity of the sky concealing the day to be.

"But jeez, that stinks!" He waves his hand in front of his nose. "You think you can get Rodney to find whatever's dead before that boat gets here? They're gonna think we're hiding bodies."

I pause a beat too long.

"You want me to go wake him?" he offers.

"No, no, I'll go bang on the shed."

"There you go. Kid can't sleep all day."

He turns to leave, adjusting his scrawny little ponytail in the opening above the snapback strap of his Fifty Mission Cap. I'm dying to cut that ponytail, but no matter how badly he could use it, I'm not quite ready to share that particular skill. I wouldn't even recommend he shave the whole lot, considering how little he has left, just tame it into a sort of

Gene Hackman fringe. With curly hair, there's something about a man keeping just a bit of it that has a certain charm. Maybe that's just me.

✂

The wind is blowing out of the northwest today, so the smell is likely coming from the dumpster beside the spar shed. The most reasonable explanation is actual rotting meat or a dead animal, but something irrational in me needs to go and check the shoreline inside The Mistake. Before I enlist Rodney, I need to know it's clear of baggage.

Rodney is the Commodore's fifteen-year-old son, who, for custodial reasons, is living here at the club this summer. When Jenny told Rodney she was moving out to BC with her new boyfriend, they had a big fight and Rodney refused to go. So the Commodore, being a bit delinquent on parental care, built Rodney an amazing loft in the spar shed, the corrugated metal hangar where we store the masts for the winter. The loft consists of a wooden sheet suspended from the ceiling, making a space about as tall as Rodney, running the upper width of the building. The platform holds a bed, a dresser, and the most recent addition: a set of free weights, since Rodney has taken an interest. You don't pass by now that you don't hear him grunting.

Having always maintained a hands-off policy with kids, I was caught off guard by Rodney. As an only child of parents living a certain lifestyle, he'd learned to make his own fun in the company of drunken adults. But when we met, and he looked up at me for the first time, his eight-year-old eyes filled with the hope that I might be different from other grownups—that I might be different enough to want to *play*—my heart clunked right out at his feet. It's not so long ago I remember wishing the same thing about my parents' friends (*Surely one of you wants to colour* ...). People who spend time around kids must build up resistance, but I had no defences at all. There we were in a secured compound bordered by water with no escape, and when Jenny would drop him by on summer days, he'd inevitably fall to my care, such as it was. I'd wake up mornings to find him sitting in The Pill's cockpit, drawing intricate puzzles filled with pictures for me to find. One time when we were fishing off the dock, he turned to me and said that I was like a brother—only better because I was a girl, but not really a girl. Being liked by him somehow outranked all grown-up approval.

But I'm not his brother anymore, because he's twigged to my place in the hierarchy. And I'm *certainly* not his mom.

I know kids have to grow up and lose faith in us, but he used to think I was so cool. When he was nine, and into "boy" things—slugs, caterpillars—I showed him David Lynch's *Eraserhead*, figuring he'd get a kick out of that slimy snake baby. It's unsettling in a special way to those of us afraid of snakes and babies. When it was over, Rodney turned to me, eyes wide, and said, "Has anyone else seen this?" He was the one who named the boats in the sailing school after David Lynch films. After that, he was hungry for anything different I could show him—bands, movies, books … Look at Tom Waits! Look at *The Wasp Factory*! But lately, he's renounced anything that makes him "weird," which also means me. I've been relegated to the things he's outgrown. Like Pooh Bear. And slugs.

On my way to the spar shed, I pick up a cigarette pack and a couple of bottle caps. I'm bending over for a Popsicle stick when I hear Rodney's sneakers crunch up behind me and stop. The sniper heat of his eyes on my ass makes me jump, and I turn to see him standing there in a striped polo shirt his mom would have given him back when it fit, and when he exclusively wore a filthy *2001: A Space Odyssey* T-shirt that he's also outgrown. The polo shirt now rides up his stovepipe torso, exposing his tight six-pack, his belly button like an ampersand. I avert my eyes. Every time I see Rodney these days, it takes a moment to orient myself—my weird little friend is now a creepy adolescent with sexual self-awareness and brand-new muscles. He used to be a chatterbox, and now he says almost nothing, apparently consumed by a private dirty joke I'd often swear is me.

"Whoooa," he says, a hint of lingering pubescent break in his mostly changed voice. "Little high-strung there?"

He's posing, hip canted, waiting for me to look at him in that tiny shirt. I look him in the face.

"Yes?"

He lifts his arms, and the shirt pulls up to his rib cage.

"What can I do for you, Rodney?"

"I need school clothes," he says.

"So ask your dad."

"Dad's a pig," he says.

"Hey!"

"I can't go to Hollister with him looking like that if Trent and those guys are there." He ruffles a thick mess of hair over his eye. "Can you just take me?"

"I thought you hated Trent and those guys."

"They're okay ..."

Without Jenny here, I'm stuck in a quasi-parental role I have no aptitude for. There's no reason for me *not* to take him to the mall. "Let me talk to your dad."

"You don't need his permission."

"I *know*. Rodney. I know." Glad to change the subject, I say, "Hey! Something stinks! Do you think you can have a look and see if something died over by the dumpsters?"

He snickers. "Sure," he says.

This is what I mean about the private dirty joke.

"Hey." He lifts his chin to the northeasterly wind. "Maybe if this picks up, we can play Windy Day later." He saunters off as I squint back suspiciously.

He hasn't wanted to play Windy Day for years. He really doesn't think I can see through his tactics, like he's the first kid to try and manipulate an adult. When I look at him now, I get wistful for the kid who showed me how, on a windy enough day, if you open up the big front door to the spar shed and the little back one, and you hang from the pull-up bar there, the force of the cross-breeze is strong enough to blow you uncontrollably back and forth. It's hilarious. The most important part of the game, though, is yelling to the other person about how windy it is. "Whoooooooooooa, that's windy!" "That's a winnnndy daaaaaaaaaaaaaaaaaaaaaaaay!" etc. At first, Rodney had to jump to reach the bar; now, he has to lift his feet off the ground or they drag—not that he uses it for anything but pull-ups anymore.

His boyhood does, though, still make the odd fading appearance. Last week, I was in the hut when I looked up from my book to see him out on the water in the Mulholland Drive, fishing. The bucolic childhood innocence of it was almost funny. And then he actually got a bite. He was so excited that he started hooting in his broken voice. As he reeled it in, he checked the shore to see if anyone had seen. The Commodore wasn't around, so I ran out and hollered and clapped and gave him a thumbs-up. What he'd caught was a good-sized mud shark. Ugly, but close to three feet long. He was so proud.

As I near The Mistake, I scan the empty shore and sigh. Of course it's not littered with trash bags; they're in my dreams. I know the difference between waking and dreaming. I pull a long stick of cedar out from under some seaweed and pierce the shoreline. The stones make a *coosh* sound. I stab my stick into the ground again and again. *Real, real, real.* I don't know why this is such a relief.

I turn back toward the mouth of the inlet as a Frers 33 powers past, heading for the marina. Hurrying along the embankment, I make out the name on its side in big blue letters: COURAGE. They're early. A ratty grey dog stands valiantly at the pulpit rail, barking its head off, and a dark-haired woman in a tangerine bikini is grasping the forestay over her head like the pole in a men's club. A beefy man in a grey T-shirt and long red drawstring shorts stands at the helm. He's wearing wraparound sunglasses and half lifts a hand in greeting to the Commodore standing on the dock.

"Ahoy!" shouts the Commodore.

"Ahoy!" says the man, and I slow my step.

That voice.

I look closer and cover my mouth with both hands. Sure enough, that's his hair, thinner and greyer, straight like pine needles, its texture burned into my memory. I jump behind a boulder on the shore, my heart thudding its way up my throat.

Mitch.

From the mist of the Fundy coast, just about to tie up here at the marina in a boat named after a song by his high school favourite band, is fucking Mitch. I wish there was someone I could share the absurdity of this with, but it would be him.

The Commodore is waiting for them, so I don't have to run up and help. I watch from my hiding spot as the woman in the bikini throws the line to the Commodore. She must be half Mitch's age. What's the appeal of a man in the throes of a midlife crisis for a young woman like her? I mean, she's like a model. How did she find her way through the mess of balding schlubs to find this one? He's been working out, I'll give him that. He used to be skinny. Now he's super jacked, up top—and only up top. The fabric of his T-shirt is stretched across his chest while his legs are like sticks.

He shuts off the engine and approaches the boat's lifeline, now secured. I can't believe the Commodore is about to make contact with him, but true to form, he reaches out a hand. It's unclear whether he wants to help Mitch over the line or introduce himself, so they hold hands for a second, then Mitch lets go, climbs over the line, and lands on the dock. They have a strange moment where they haven't shaken hands, but they've held hands, so the Commodore boldly reaches again for Mitch's hand and shakes it. Of course he does.

The woman has made her way to the stern to guide the dog onto the decking, where it instantly whizzes. The Commodore reaches out to help the woman over the lifeline, and she shakes his hand, then realizes he's trying to help her and steps across. She waves a hand in front of her nose, and the Commodore says something that makes her laugh. Then he directs a finger to Mitch's chest. I was so distracted that I didn't notice the handwritten Tragically Hip lettering on Mitch's shirt. I know—because I'm an expert now—that's it's the cover of the *Day for Night* album and the shirt is from the 1995 tour.

I can't hide forever, but I can't think of how to act. Do I treat him like a stranger? High school acquaintance? Or do I come right out and make it known that he's a sexual predator who feels bad enough about it to try to pay for forgiveness? Mitch is no fool. I assume his own well-being tops his list of priorities, so he'll probably want just as badly to keep our acquaintance a secret. God knows, we've both got reason.

I take a breath and go in neutral. The Commodore has pulled off his cap and his head is bowed, which means he's still talking about The Tragically Hip.

"Gonna miss him …" he says.

I stab my stick in the gravel and the Commodore turns. "Lou!" The dog gives a big bark and trots over to sniff me, tags jingling.

"Lou, this is Mitch. Mitch, Louise, our Dockmaster. But I'm sure you must know each other, both being from Trannah and all." The Commodore says it the way people who hate Toronto say it, and also the way Torontonians say it. "Don't you all know each other?"

The man I cradled in my arms and forgave stands before me now, mechanically chewing gum, his face frozen in a leer of mastication. I can't see his eyes behind his glasses, which gives his face a cold, Terminator effect, something he's almost certainly striving for. I spend too long trying to read his unreadable expression, neither of us responding, and the Commodore twigs.

"Wait, *do you*?"

"Oh …" I say, jumping in, "didn't you go to Mimico Collegiate?"

He cocks his head, sizing me up. "Yeah," he says. Then, thoughtfully, like he's really putting his mind to it, "Did we know each other?"

The Commodore looks like he's won the lottery. "You two went to high school together? Are you shitting me???"

"We were in different years …" I say, my pulse speeding up.

Mitch shakes his head apologetically, like he just can't place me. "That was a big school." He shrugs.

"Ho-ho, maybe Louise had a little crush on you," says the Commodore in his teasing voice, and Mitch snickers back with a rancid delight.

"Hey, I don't know." He holds up his hands, feigning modesty.

I'm trembling by the time the woman in the bikini reaches out and firmly shakes my hand. "I'm Grace," she says, smiling guilelessly with both sets of gums. I catch myself gawking. She's got his shining black eyes and a widow's peak like a Romanian baroness, and now that we're close up, I see how young she really is. "I'm his daughter."

Grace. All my fight drains away and a slurry liquefies in my chest. The urge to put pants on her, to throw her in the car and get her far away from him, is overwhelming. But here she is, his daughter, with her confidence and her long, long legs … What I wouldn't have given for her self-possession at that age. Something in her young womanhood triggers the wisdom of my thirty-eight years, and I channel Constance.

"You're not even twenty, are you?"

"I'm nineteen."

"Hey, she's legal!" says the Commodore, and we all stare. He continues, unfazed, "I mean for wobbly pops. You all coming up the clubhouse to watch the show? Pour one out for the Great Man?"

"There, Dad," announces Grace. "You don't have to watch it on your phone. He's been whining this whole trip about missing that show."

"Long as I can bring my buddy, here," says Mitch, awkwardly pulling focus to the dog like it's his security blanket. He makes a show of thumping the animal's flanks. "This is Program, my best buddy. Isn't he? Who's my guy?"

It's a lot to take in. "Hi, Program," I say. "Where'd you get that name?"

"That's the name he had when I got him from the shelter. Isn't it? Isn't it, boy? Isn't it, Pro? But you're not stuck there anymore, are you? Nooooo."

"Anyway, Lou can show you to your slip," says the Commodore. "Anything you need, this is your Girl Friday, right here." He slaps my arm in an odd gesture of pride.

I wouldn't normally let something like "Girl Friday" go unremarked, but I'll spare him this time. Still, I don't care for the hired-labour feel of this exchange, despite my actually being hired labour.

"Right on," says Mitch, in a studiously indifferent tone. There's an elsewhereness to him that feels like it must be a lot of work. He climbs aboard and extends a hand to me. Ignoring his hand, I step on, suddenly self-conscious of the weight displacement of the Courage when my sneaker leaves the dock. Program and Grace jump on too, and the Commodore waves us off like we're going to war. I point Mitch toward their empty berth and my head starts to hum.

"Brrr," says Grace, heading for the cabin. "I'm going to get my sweater."

"S'wondering when you might put something on ..." Mitch says pointedly.

She rolls her eyes at me as she passes, and I brighten at the feminine rapport.

When it's just the two of us in the cockpit, Mitch fixes me with his cold, empty grin. He barely moves his mouth to speak. "So we're good, right?"

"How d'you mean?"

"We don't need to go yapping to her." He nods to the cabin.

"About what?"

"Yeah, I figured you might not want it out there either."

"What are we talking about, exactly?"

He snickers. "Your, uh, unsavoury job?"

I gape back at him just as he hits one of the pilings making the turn into the berth. "Shit," he says, sharply turning the wheel. "If that scratched the lettering ..."

The boat's sudden veering pulls us close, and I reflexively shove him before jumping up to fend us off on the starboard side. Grace climbs out the companionway in a flax-coloured cable-knit cardigan and makes her way to the foredeck with me.

"Jesus, Dad, watch the pilings."

I'm apoplectic as I jump onto the dock and secure their line. I face them, turning my full attention to her. "The show starts at eight thirty, but the bar's open at four. You can fuel up in the morning on your way out. If you need anything, let me know. I'll be around the yard."

"Hey," says Grace, just as I'm heading away, fuming. "Do you and the Commodore want to come by for wobbly pops before the show? Since I'm of age and all?" she asks.

"Nah, Grace, she's got work to do," Mitch says.

The sour ambient waves of Mitch not wanting me there are as good a reason as any for me to say yes; his wanting me to refrain from yapping to his daughter makes me want to all the more.

She comes up to the lifeline and reaches out both hands. "Please," she says. "I've been alone with my dad for close to three weeks. I haven't seen another girl. Please?"

"Hey!" he says.

"Say you'll come!" She gives me desperate eyes.

Now that he's awakened it, I'm abuzz with the chemical kick of this strand of anger; I can't assault him, but I can ride the thrill of wanting to, a feeling at once nostalgic, exhilarating, and life-affirming. Look how it's flourished in my heart.

"All right, but only if it's to save you from your dad."

✂

Back aboard The Pill, I make a rum and Coke, take a long drink, and lay my forehead on the table.

Under what moon was I born that this moron gets to wash ashore every so often and upend me? While he gets to cruise through life with his yacht and his beautiful daughter who believes he's just a regular dad.

Grace, though … I assume she's mostly a product of her mom. He shouldn't even be around girls at all. Though they seem pretty close—would she travel two thousand kilometres at sea with a dad she hated? When I scour the depths of my soul for what's irritating me most right now about them, it's that I don't want him enjoying the pleasure of that father-daughter relationship; I don't want her to love him as much as I loved mine.

I could use a quick sail, but I have to set up the projector and stock the bar before the show. I wonder what Grace drinks …

A knock comes on the hatch above, followed by a loud, "LOU!"

I've never once locked the companionway. There's a chance it would hurt the Commodore's feelings if he knew I felt unsafe enough to lock my boat. But at least we've established knocking.

"Come in."

The brim of his cap and a crack of sunshine peek through the hatch. "Got a minute?"

"'Course."

He takes out the boards and steps over the threshold. The fog's lifted right on time, and a glorious day has burned its way through. The Commodore's cautious Tevas make way for his permanently browned ankles, and I get an image of my dad in short shorts, standing at the barbecue, blackening T-bones. The similarities between them are hard to avoid. I didn't have the pleasure of seeing the Commodore in his prime. He's always had the beer gut, he says, but a certain charm and an all-access backstage pass go a long way.

He sits on the top step, surveying the cabin, holding two stuffed manila folders in his lap.

"You can come in," I say.

"Enh, it takes a minute," he says. "I think of all the times I cheated on her in here. God, I was a tit." His eyes wander morosely around the cabin. He quit tech work and bought the marina when Jenny said she'd had enough of the life. The Pill was supposed to fix their marriage and give them something to do as a family once Rodney was born. Instead, the Commodore spent more time drinking at the club with the members than he did at home. As far as women were concerned, he told me he just wasn't built to pass up an opportunity, and the comings and goings of the members and their wives were much as you might expect in a Margaritaville-style adult playground. Finally, one day Jenny stuffed his car with his belongings, drove it to the front gates, locked the keys inside, and took a cab home. That's when the Commodore moved into his office full-time.

"Jeez, this thing …" He shakes his head. "It was every-where. Everywhere …"

The *thing* he means is Alanis Morissette's *Jagged Little Pill*. It was the biggest-selling record in Canada while he and Jenny were falling in love, and it's the boat's namesake. For all his love of the Hip, *Jagged Little Pill* is still his favourite album. He can't sell the boat on account of the memories, but he can't live aboard it for the same reason.

"I'd really rather not think of all the times you cheated on her in here," I say. "Okay?"

He nods and shuffles down the steps. "So what's the problem?"

"What?"

His liquor-trained eyes speed to my glass. "We're having these? At this hour?"

"We're adults," I say.

"Don't mind if I do." He goes to the galley to make himself a drink in one of my seagull tumblers.

"You did have a crush on that guy, didn't you?" he says, clattering in the cupboard.

I put my head in my hands. "Please stop."

He laughs. "You don't have to explain. Guy's a bit of a dick, though. Maybe he'll loosen up with a cocktail." The Commodore rummages in the ice chest.

I sigh. "He is a dick. But we've been invited for drinks before the show with him and his amazing daughter."

"Ooh! All right."

"Try not to be a dirty old man."

"She's quite something."

"Isn't she?"

"Jeez, having a girl like that, you'd be worried all the time."

"Because of you."

"Because of us, yes." He stirs his drink with a finger, then slurps off the finger and lays his hands on his messy folders. There's a pen in his shirt pocket.

"I've been getting my affairs in order," he says. "It's been years since Jenny, and … I guess it's time. I've been keeping things like they were, just in case. But that's …"

"You're doing this today?"

"Has to get done."

"Great Man?"

He nods. It's not the worst thing that he's acquainting himself at this age with his own mortality, or that it's thanks to Gord Downie, who's offering a master class in it. Gord has been revealing himself unreservedly to the whole country in his most vulnerable moment. As a man beloved by men, he's stripping away all the bullshit self-preservation and lone-wolf suffering (what Constance would call the Fallacy of Autarky), laying himself wide open and showing us that he's sad and scared. And what the Great Man wants to do tonight, if you can imagine, is sing and dance for us one last time, while we watch him die. If that's not hardcore, I don't know what is.

"Yeah, I guess it's time to think about … my legacy."

"Guy …"

"There's a chance, Louise, that I've been a rotter."

"Well. What do they say? 'Quit wishing for a better past'? You're not dead, you know. You're a good person *now*."

He sighs. "All right, look, let's get this out of the way. I just want to make sure you and Rodney are taken care of."

"Oh," I say. "You don't have to worry about me."

"No, no, just …" He looks into his seagull tumbler and pushes a stapled stack of papers across the table. "I've named you executor," he says. "And I'd like you to have the boat."

"Oh," I say. "Wow. Okay. Thanks."

"Now, everything else goes to Rodney, but he doesn't get it until he's eighteen."

"Okay."

"And he's going to need a guardian."

I wait for the rest, but he says nothing.

"Oh. Oh … No, I don't think that's how kids work. He has a mom."

"He doesn't want to live out there, Lou. He hates Geoff and the whole idea of BC. He wouldn't last. With all that fleece? Jenny doesn't want him out there anyway—or Geoff doesn't. He'd be miserable. If he can just stay here and finish out school … You'd barely have to do anything. Just make sure he gets fed and catches the bus. He loves you. I am asking this as a favour. You know he needs no supervision."

The fact that the Commodore believes that boy needs no supervision is one of the reasons I should say yes. Also,

Rodney doesn't love me *anymore*, but now isn't the time to sulk about that.

"Just think about it. Please."

"You want him to remember you fondly? Spend some time with him."

"He hates me."

"He's supposed to hate you, he's a teenager. But he'll feel bad about it in ten years or so. And so will you."

"If I live to see it …"

"Hey! Stop talking like that. If you're giving me this boat, you can't say those things in here. My rules. Furthermore, you're aware of what Rodney's going through, yes?"

He squints.

"He's fifteen … certain changes are …"

"Oh, huh." He lifts a hand.

"Has he even had the—birds and—"

"They get that from the internet now."

"I'm serious."

"Or school. Honestly, parents don't do that anymore."

"This is dad work. He needs to be told, on his way to manhood, by you, certain things. Especially where girls are concerned."

"… Such as?"

"That they're his fucking equals. And about consent, respect, not being a predator …"

"Phew. He's going to call me a hypocrite. I can only imagine the things Jenny's told him."

"Who better to guide him than someone who's already made the mistakes?" I say. "No lamb is so precious as the one who strayed from the flock and found his way back."

"Who said that?"

"... Jesus?"

"Well, I still fuck it up all the time."

"You fucked it up with 'Girl Friday' there earlier, but other than that, you've done good today."

"Girl Friday isn't okay?"

"It implies my servitude."

"Shit."

"Also, I'm not a girl."

"You guys don't like that?"

"It's like calling me a child. It saps my authority."

"Huh."

"Look, Rodney needs you. You have no idea of your influence. Also, he needs school clothes. He wants to look *normal*. Put on something with sleeves and take him to the mall."

"Boy, that's really been more of a Jenny thing."

"Not anymore."

He gazes through the galley hatch contemplatively.

"Hey," I say. "I have work to do. And I have to nap. You're messing with my schedule."

"Understood," he says, and gulps down the rest of his drink. He closes the folder and sets the pen from his pocket on top. "The executor and guardianship stuff has the pink stickies. Give it a read. I'll see you later for green ones."

He drops his glass in the sink, then picks it back up, washes it, and sets it in the drying rack. As I say, we've come a long way.

>%

The Commodore is a young sixty-four and isn't going anywhere, but I haven't given much thought to what might happen if he did. I haven't considered that, without him, it's just me and Rodney. I mean, I haven't thought of any of this.

The afternoon breeze sends a whiff of putrescence through the cabin. Rodney obviously hasn't dealt with the garbage, and I don't have the fortitude to wait him out. Now I'm thinking about Grace's nose.

I blink up at the sky through the hatch, marvelling at how the crystal blue and the tendrils of fluffy cloud drifting past up there exist in the same world where I have to be polite over cocktails with a man who used me as a sexual gag to amuse his friend.

As the afternoon warms, the smell over the yard keeps maturing. I open the tops of the three steel garbage bins at the north side of the building and find them filled with the usual six-pack rings, Triscuit boxes, and little shopping bags full of galley trash, so I turn and follow my nose to the open door of the spar shed. I stick my head inside and take another sniff—it's definitely coming from in there. The shed is dark and empty—or so it seems, until a shuffling sound comes from way up in the loft. I figure it's Rodney lifting weights. I'm about to bang on the door like we agreed when I hear a sustained moan. I freeze. The shuffling stops.

"Hello?" honks Rodney.

I silently back out the door and walk away briskly, head lowered, then speed up, trying to outrun the mental image and block the sound that's playing on a loop in my head.

><

I've always liked Jenny. It's a shame we've only got to know each other through her occasional visits to pick up or drop off Rodney. Given the Commodore's behaviour on the premises while they were married, she's got no fondness for this place and doesn't hang around. When she's here, she watches the women. She's always cordial with me, though it seems tinged with a sad inevitability. Jenny was the girl the Commodore thought he could never win, then won, then spent years proving he didn't deserve. I don't know why she stuck it out for so long, but she certainly gave that marriage a shot. She designs baby clothes and has just launched a four-storey, open-concept, exposed-brick production facility in Vancouver, where her 0–6X designs are produced by a happy, well-paid staff. There's talk of expansion to the Netherlands. It's hard not to envy her life; she has a Lauren Hutton elegance I could never pull off.

The last time I saw her was at the beginning of the summer, when she dropped Rodney off.

"I adore him, you know," she said as we watched him drag his bedding from her car across the parking lot. "Rod, that's on the ground, bud!" she called. He nodded, carrying on. "More than life itself. I'm not leaving him here because I don't want him to live with me and Geoff. It's so beautiful out there, and it would do him so much good. I'm leaving him here because it's what *he* wants."

The Commodore walked by, proudly carrying Rodney's twin mattress over his head. He gave a flex for Jenny as he passed.

"I mean, who wouldn't want to live here like Jimmy Buffett with that idiot?" She eyed him grudgingly. "Rodney's found the option with the fewest restrictions, and Bruce feels flattered he got chosen without trying. Well, getting what you want can be an important lesson, and it's one they'll learn together. Let *him* try parenting for a bit."

"He's making an effort," I said. "He built him that loft."

She levelled a withering are-you-serious face at me.

"He set him up with the internet," I said. "And he hates the internet. Honestly, Jenny. He feels bad all the time. He never stops talking about it."

"It's a start," she said. "But look," here she actually pointed her finger, "don't you take this on. He doesn't just get to pass his son off to the nearest adult who finds it cute that he can't seem to grow up himself ... Rodney, pick this *up*, please, bud!"

✂

The projector screen is already set up when I get to the clubhouse, clearly the work of the Commodore. The clubhouse bar consists of four long tables with benches and a few stools at the little lift-up countertop. You can keep stock behind there, but no one tends it. We have an honour system everyone forgets about when they're drinking, but around Christmastime I'll start getting envelopes of cash, fifties and hundreds. It's funny being sentimental about a currency denomination, but I still love a nice stack of Bordens and Mackenzie Kings.

The clubhouse doesn't get much use, considering how much more fun it is to drink in your own cockpit. Parties usually take place over the decks of a few neighbouring boats, or on the concrete slab between the docks, but it's nice when the members all gather in the clubhouse, if only because the Commodore gets to hold court in his spot in front of the window.

While I'm setting up the laptop and speakers, I play the CBC. They've dedicated the whole day to Gord Downie and The Tragically Hip. Every single talk segment is someone telling a story about the time they met Gord and how he remembered their name years later, or it's some musical expert dissecting "Bobcaygeon" and "Nautical Disaster," looking at the complexity of the melodies and unlikeliness of the chord progressions. There are segments about the significance of the lyrics, Downie's Canadian imagery and literary references. The news itself consists largely of stories about community viewing events set up for people to watch the broadcast all over the country at rinks and restaurants and movie theatres, and private screenings, where people are bringing their TVs out to their driveways and inviting the neighbours. And every half hour, when the news report repeats the words "the band's front man" and "terminal brain cancer," they hit just as hard as the first time. I'm curious how Mitch is handling it.

I finish loading twenty cases of Alpine out back, fill the three big metal troughs with bottles, and dump in bag after bag of ice. I've visited the liquor store every day this week to buy all of their White Star rum, stocking sixteen bottles in the dry goods closet. The members should be able to arrive here ready for cocktail hour, and not worry about anything else for the rest of the night until they stumble off to sleep in their boats.

Out in the yard, they're already starting to pull into the parking lot, cracking beers right there and toasting. Leslie Baxter is crying. Dean Pearce's Subaru is playing "Blow at High Dough" with all the windows open, and Juan Ferrara's Prius is playing "In a World Possessed by the Human Mind." They're duelling: early versus late Hip. The Commodore is directing traffic, the Tall Green One aloft like a conductor's baton. Dean waves a hand in front of his nose, reminding me that I have to go back up to Rodney's shed. I swear, as I look up at it from where I stand in the clubhouse, I can hear the demonic score from *The Omen*.

I tighten up a light fixture in the stairwell on my way down, dawdling. I change the silica sand in the ashtray outside, combing it with my fingers to create parallel rivulets like a prayer garden.

Finally, standing again outside the shed, I scan the darkness inside. I hold my breath and pound on the open door.

"Rodney?"

An echo rings out. Nothing. I try again.

"RODNEY!"

He can't be in there. I take a step inside, halving the music outside. Jesus, that smell … For an instant, I wonder if it could just be the unholy ecosystem of his sneakers, but no. This is different.

The frosted glow of the skylight over his bed defines the outline of his pungent lair. This is the first time I've ever climbed this ladder, because we have an understanding about privacy. He's left me no choice. I put my hands on the side rails and look up.

"Bud?"

I pause on the first rung, bracing for anything, and climb. When I reach the platform, I tenderly plant a foot on the creaking plywood and wonder how much weight the cables can hold.

Rodney's desk is cluttered but nothing looks too rotten. His garbage can is full, but not in active decomposition. His bed is a mess of sheets, which is nothing new, but as I crawl toward it, I notice a rounded contour and stop.

"Rodney?"

The form doesn't move. I kneel next to the bed, reach out a finger, and poke the shape. It's dense and still. I poke it again. Nothing. Wincing, I pull the edge of the covers toward me. Whatever it is, it's wrapped tightly in his duvet, but I manage to create a little opening to expose something dark. It smells exactly like the sweet, putrid core of what's been blowing around in the breeze. I hold my breath and pull at the opening to reveal a mouth. With teeth. I jump back with the duvet in my hand, which spins the thing from its swaddling. It lands on the floor with a thump. I let out a quick scream.

Lying heavily on the plywood is the mud shark. An icy hand wrings my heart as I kneel before it, my mind spinning for an explanation that squares with the kid I know. Anything. And the only one that makes any sense is that, as I've suspected for a while now, the Rodney I know is dead. The invader that's taken over has moved in full-time, and he has no shame or limits. A sense of loss starts to sink in, but it doesn't get far before my nerves remind me I'm still on the invader's turf, tampering with his kill. I snap back to prime directive and concentrate on disposal.

Shaking, I wrap the thing in the foul comforter. It's probably ten pounds. I'd wonder how he got it up here, but I'd say this new Rodney is capable of anything. I'm still on my knees, readying to stand, and I fling it over my shoulder when I hear him quack from the far side of the shed.

"Hello?"

I close my eyes and wait for the echo to ebb.

"… Hi," I say.

"What—what are you—?" His footsteps speed across the floor. He appears at the top of the ladder with a green garbage bag balled up in his hand. The mask of his face darkens.

"I know, I know, I'm sorry, but Rodney—you can smell it everywhere."

He climbs the top two rungs and his eyes fix me stonily.

"Oh, can this hold both of us?" I say. "I'm not sure it can …"

The boards creak as he steps forward, lowering himself to sit cross-legged opposite me, his knees inches from mine. He's completely still, his eyes burning into me. I pull back, trying to create some distance between us, my adrenalin rising.

He barely moves his lips. "You're. Not. Supposed. To. Be. Up. Here," he says in a voice a full octave lower than usual.

The systems kick in and my fingers curl into fists. "Rodney …" I half whisper, the name a hiccup. He cranes forward just enough to fill the space between us, and I reach for his dresser behind me, flailing my arms like I'm shaking him off. Even though it only lasted a few seconds, being restrained by Spence has left me with an especial fear of confinement, just as being spoken to in a quiet, intense tone of voice triggers a reflex. If Rodney comes any closer, I'm going to hit him. I'll send him over the edge, and he'll split his head open on the concrete floor. He keeps his face inches from mine, and I can't think which of us is going to end this, but someone has to do something. The words are right there in my mouth.

"What was it doing in your bed?" I whisper.

He leans in closer and parts his lips. I'm readying a foot to strike, when the Commodore's voice rises up from below.

"Hey, Bud?"

Rodney doesn't move.

"Yeah, Dad," he says, without taking his eyes from me.

"Hey, just wondered if you have time for a quick chat."

Rodney's face slackens as he considers me coolly. I swallow another hiccup.

"Just take a sec," says the Commodore.

I give him a *Go* with my eyes.

"Uh … yeah, Dad, hang on. I'll be right down." He climbs over the side and starts down the ladder. Before his head disappears, he glances up at me and smirks.

"Jesus, Rodney. What's that smell?"

"Oh, it's a dead rabbit out by the trash. I was just going to bury it."

"See you do. People are starting to show up," says the Commodore as they wander toward the door together.

When their voices are out of range, I slowly uncurl the fingers on each hand, the left one crunched in a kind of claw. I can barely hold the edges of the garbage bag as I scoop the shark into it, throw it over my shoulder, and scramble down to the ground.

The parking lot is too loud and the members too distracted to notice me sneaking past—not to mention that the sight of me with a garbage bag is utterly unremarkable. Only Dr. Harmon spots me and lifts her beer. I lift the bag.

Moving speedily around the edge of the yard, I collect a couple of big rocks and load them with the shark into the Eraserhead, tied up at the diesel dock. No one glances as I raise her sails and bring her around the spit. Only once I'm under sail can I finally release the air from my lungs, but my heart still hammers as I round the bend of The Mistake. The black plastic mass sits ominously at my feet. I luff the sails, tie the bag, and pitch it over the side, my nerves still jittering as the surface burbles. I hold up my hands, trembling from fear or rage or both, and then I plunge them into the water, rinsing furiously, pulling up my soaked hoodie sleeves to splash my forearms, scrubbing until my tendons seize.

With no room to stretch out, I slide down and recline in the bottom of the cockpit with my legs dangling over the stern. The stinking air clears and a version of tranquility settles in. With each eastbound puff of cloud that traverses overhead, I try to calm my mind, but the shark and Rodney's cold expression produce steady waves of horror, like a migraine rolling in. I squeeze my eyes shut tight. I'm his pigeon. He knows full well he can reach right into me and turn the knobs, and this new Rodney finds it funny.

If I were Moitessier, I'd sail straight out to the harbour and just follow the coast. I'd dock from time to time for supplies and carry on. Moitessier would have written them a note tell-ing them not to wait up and catapulted it to shore in a metal tube. But that's not how we deal with problems, now, is it?

I shake out my hands.

Breathe.

The wind catches and releases the crumpled sails, and I poke the tiller with my foot, viewing it, as I often do, as a long nose with a screw for an eye on either side.

I kick the nose. The eye stares back.

As I return to the club, a gentle puff of exhaust from the Irving Oil refinery is the only cloud in an endlessly still blue sky. The wind has picked up and the air is noticeably more breathable, though no one does notice, as a few early barbecues dominate with the smell of burgers.

On the way to The Pill, I check the yard. Grace's laugh pierces the air, and I turn to see her standing on the dock beside the Courage, with Rodney. "Oh, you're adorable, I love you," she says, playfully pushing him. He playfully pushes her back, making her playfully push *him* back, and a low siren whines in my head. I've never seen Rodney even speak to a girl, let alone push one, but he's like an iceberg, all the action lurking beneath the surface. Program barks excitedly beside them.

Rodney laughs and pushes Grace again, harder, and everything slows down. Without stopping to think, I launch a foot toward them, but Grace has already caught herself, laughing—HAHAHA—and reaches an arm up to hug him. But instead of hugging him, she wraps herself around behind him, hits out with her other hand so his hip kicks forward, his knees buckle, and he falls onto them. She's left holding him in a headlock. I skid to a stop in the gravel. She holds him just long enough to deliver a flurry of spankings atop his head, like he's her bratty little brother. When Rodney extricates himself, his face is crimson. He glares back for a second before morphing back into himself—whatever that is—and he shows his hands like she's won. He leaves a wide berth as he passes her, playing like he's afraid, and makes for the loft, adjusting his shorts.

Throughout all this, Mitch has been sitting in the cockpit, sunglasses on, typing on his phone, then scrolling, then shaking his head and typing again. Having never witnessed him interact with a mobile device, I note how like a grooming monkey he looks. I wonder if Rodney's flirting is getting to him—it is his daughter. Does he know she's a streetfighter? But he doesn't even look up. I indulge a quick fantasy of Grace and me beating him up together, as a team.

I take a few steps forward to get a better look at his screen and catch the unmistakable blue of Facebook. In my mind, he still lives in 1994, but he's been out there all this time adapting to the same world as everyone else.

"Evenin', Master," says the Commodore, saluting me with the Tall Green One on his way down the steps from the parking lot. He only calls me Master when he's in an exceptionally good mood, into the green ones, or both.

"Evenin'," I say carefully.

"Did you know your high school buddy's daughter is taking Nautical Science at Cape Breton U?"

"Wow."

"Quite a young woman."

"She is. She just kicked Rodney's ass here a second ago."

"Ha! *She* did?"

"Put him in a headlock. She's like MMA."

"Well, well!"

"So you and the boy had a little chat?"

"Yeah," he says. "And get this: he *wanted* to talk, but he didn't want to ask me because he finds me intimidating. Can you believe that?"

I narrow my eyes.

"Imagine ... So we went over the basics, and turns out no one's got more respect for girls—"

"—than Rodney."

He shrugs.

"He said those words."

"Basically."

How do I tell him? Look at him. "Mm."

"I also mentioned the will. I didn't think he'd be so interested in the club, but he may just want to work here like his old man. You two could run it together."

I say nothing.

"*Intimidating.* Can you imagine, Lou? I had no idea."

I take a moment to appreciate the depth of Rodney's cunning. I'm not about to hurt the Commodore's feelings by saying anything to the contrary, since he's so pleased with himself.

"As always, I have you to thank." He takes a big, proud drink. "It's different when they're yours, Louise," he continues as we walk. "I mean, he's *mine.*" He pats his chest. "Flesh and blood, you know? But also," he glances around, "Jenny isn't happy out there. Rod says things aren't working out with Geoff."

"Oh, Guy …"

"I know, I know, but still … I can't say I'm not happy to hear it. Also, Rodney says that stink from earlier was a dead rabbit over by the shed. He's got it under control."

When we reach The Pill, I turn. "Well, that's great. I guess I'll see you in a bit with our new friends, then?"

"Looking forward to the hijinks." He salutes me with his cap brim and saunters away down the dock, the toes of his Tevas splayed in his childlike gait. Watching him go, I catch sight of Rodney peeking out from the entrance to the shed. I take out the boards and push back the hatch. He's still there.

I lock the hatch. As I grip the padlock, my blood starts to thump and I back into the settee, curling up on my side with my knees to my chest. I pull my hood over my head. Then a beach towel. Then I disinter a sweater mashed between the cushions at the other end and put that over my head. And I drift, listening for the rattle of the latch.

✄

The Eraserhead's bow cuts the rippled black surface. I'm at the helm. Sitting in the foredeck with his back to me is a tiny man in a dark-red suit. He's looking out over the harbour. I say, "Hello?" and he turns to me with a gleeful look. It's the Man from Another Place, from *Twin Peaks*, the one who speaks backward and appears to Agent Cooper in dreams. His red shirt matches his suit.

The man leans forward, and the subtitles at the bottom of my dream play out in his halting speech, "Take care … of … him."

"Who?"

He gestures to a seafoam-green Gore-Tex duffle bag in the cockpit between us. I grip the tiller. He extends his hand toward the bag. A black Patagonia label is visible on the top.

"For her." He emphasizes each word with his wide eyes, then jumps up on deck, smooths his hair across his forehead, and does a few jagged dance steps before he pitches himself sideways into black waters that close up like tar around him.

The wind blows cold on the back of my neck, and I watch the ripples broadcast from our location, pulsing out in perpetuity from where the man splashed in, so it looks like he's hovering just beneath the surface. The Mistake is eerily quiet, a stillness breached by the sound of the bag unzipping itself. Its serrated mouth grins with the jagged teeth of the mud shark, then opens a little more, releasing Spence's laugh. I grab both handles and hold them together, but the mouth blows open with a guffaw.

"Let me ouuuuuuuuuuuut!"

I catch the zipper tab and pull it closed, the bag's contents rustling with hilarity, and strenuously pitch it. The boat rocks and I crouch low to stabilize, my fists clutched to my chest. I peek over the edge. The bag lies on its side, bobbing defiantly, a happy rumpus within.

I paddle over with my hand until I'm next to the bag and reach into my pocket for my Mizutanis. "Hey," I say, poking the bag. When I push it down, it bobs back up, and then it's Rodney's little-boy voice. "Whooooooooooooa, that sure is windy!" the honk of his laugh curdling into a snicker. I position myself overtop the bag and bring the points down hard. A shriek escapes, and I stab harder, faster, reaching farther over the side, heeling the Eraserhead so the bumper strip dips beneath the surface, and we start to capsize. I slide into the frigid water, undeterred, and as the hull turtles I pull the bag closer so I'm on top of it, stabbing, stabbing, stabbing, until I'm wide awake, punching the settee.

✂

With my glass in one hand and a tin of smoked oysters in my pocket, I creak along the boards, not too fast, not too slow. Back when I was an aggressor, I'd psych myself up for shows before I walked in by pretending I was Henry Rollins. I'd mentally embody him, thick-necked and short-tempered, and respond to the world the way I felt he would. No one knows I'm doing this as I approach the Courage.

The Commodore is sitting at the helm. Whether he's imposing his status or it's just the seat that feels most natural to him, whenever he visits someone else's boat he sits in the captain's spot. It's amazing what he gets away with.

"Lou!" He's spotted me.

"Hey," says Grace, then she turns to her father and gives him a kick. Mitch lowers his leg, making room for me to sit across from him, and in his slippery movement I can see he's just a little drunk. He's still wearing sunglasses.

"Here's some more of these," I say, smiling with just my mouth as I hand him my tin.

Next to the already open smoked oysters on the table sits a tub of cream cheese and a box of Triscuits: the single acceptable way to eat a smoked oyster. I attribute the culinary acumen to Grace.

"Those things'll make you horny," says the Commodore. "You watch out."

"What can I get you?" Mitch reaches for my glass with his phony smile, like I'll go along if he sets the tone.

"Rum's good," I say. There's a bottle of Captain Morgan's on the table as well as a half-full low-calorie vodka cooler. Grace is holding an Alpine.

"Pepsi okay?" asks Mitch.

"It happens," I say, and he chuckles, loading a fistful of

ice from the cooler into my glass. We're friends now that he's had a few drinks. "By the way," I say, like a friend would, "you want to be careful who sees you drinking those things. Once you get to the clubhouse, make it easy on yourself and switch to Alpine."

"I got told already." Mitch nods up at the Commodore, who bows his head in acknowledgement. "I'm on a protein thing," he says, "so I can't take the carbs. Like, I can't drink this stuff." He nods to the can of Pepsi he's pouring from, thinking he's meeting me on my level with this diet talk. "Too much sugar."

"Aha," I say, checking Grace, who doesn't seem to find her father's low-carb talk boring or stupid. I have to assume she's had an earful of it with just the two of them on that boat. I'm shocked he'd be seen with a less-than-masculine drink, but it looks like his concern for his physical beauty wins out over his need for macho confirmation. Interesting.

He hands me my glass. His chest is comically broad and his neck probably thicker than he wants, while his little calves are tender and white and remind me of veal. His biceps look like mangoes, the skin over them soft and thin. If we were shipwrecked and it came down to it, I'd probably eat one, but I'll bet they're chewy from the gym, and I might do better to start with the calves.

"Louise."

"Hmm?"

They're holding out their drinks.

"Gord," says the Commodore solemnly.

"Gord."

We toast.

Mitch glances down at his phone, then picks it up and scrolls.

"Dad," says Grace.

He hits something on the screen, shaking his head. "It's just ... it's a ... puppy mill. They make me so ..."

"Okay," says Grace, palm open.

"I'm sending you a petition," he says, tapping the phone before handing it to her.

"I'll sign it later, Dad. We have guests."

The Commodore waits a bit, then charges on. "So Cape Breton U! Your girl's a proper mariner! You must be a proud man."

Grace gives her father a told-you-so look.

"Yeah," says Mitch. "Sure."

"Jeez," says the Commodore. "Any kid who knows what they want at that age has my respect. I *still* don't know."

"Hear that, Dad? I've got his *respect*."

"Yup," says Mitch, patting the dog.

Well, I'm certainly uncomfortable, but the Commodore soldiers on.

"So, what do you do with that?" he asks Grace. "Coast Guard? Ferry operator? Pirate?"

"Mmmm, I'm not sure yet," she says. "Coast Guard is all power; I want to sail. Tall ships, if I can. A lot of kids in my program graduate and go all over the Mediterranean and Caribbean to crew, which sounds awesome. I want to sail around the world."

The Commodore slaps his knee. My heart is bursting with all the pride her father is for some reason withholding.

Grace glances back at her dad with a mix of irritation and warmth. "We've had a boat since I was born. We spent every summer on it." Mitch says nothing. "He taught me to chart a route on a map, a paper map, when I was six."

Mitch is still scratching Program.

"Remember you used to lift me up so I could steer?"

Mitch finally cracks and lifts both arms. "You couldn't reach the edges of the wheel, so you held the inside spokes like this."

"I always knew I'd live on the water," she continues. "Watching my dad go to work in an office every day, I knew I couldn't live like that. It's not natural."

"It's nice when you can set the example of how not to be, eh?" the Commodore says to Mitch, seizing the opportunity to try to relate.

"Least I'm good for something," he says.

"So when I came home for the summer, Dad and I decided to sail me back to school along the St. Lawrence."

"That takes weeks," says the Commodore. "You guys must get along pretty good to pull that off without killing each other."

"We do." Grace responds for them both.

He gives her a look. "Well ..." he says, "her mom and me split earlier this year, so, uh, it was a good time to get away."

There we go.

"Sorry to hear it," says the Commodore.

"Ah, you know ... We had a good run. And we got this one." He nods to Grace.

"Now Mom says he's free to have his midlife crisis," she says sweetly.

"Oh, you'll love it!" says the Commodore. "I bought a marina with mine! You gonna get yourself a motorcycle? Tattoo?"

Grace snorts. "Oh, he's got one of those ..."

Mitch huffs through his nose.

"Ooh!" says the Commodore.

"I was a stupid kid," he says.

I can't disagree.

Grace gives her hands a big clap. "Oh, I shouldn't have, I'm sorry," she says, covering her mouth to contain an explosion of laughter.

"Well, we're gonna have to ..." says the Commodore judiciously.

Mitch stands up, turns around, and lifts the bottom of his T-shirt to reveal a blurry Looney Tunes Tasmanian Devil on his lower back, atop the words NO ENTRY and a thick blue arrow pointing down the waistband of his shorts.

I'm speechless.

"Right?" says Grace.

"Sweet Jesus …" murmurs the Commodore. "What would ever …?"

Mitch takes a drink. "I know. I was twenty-one."

"Twenty-one is not exactly a kid," says the Commodore.

"He was older than me," says Grace opening the ice chest in the stern and gamely reaching for another beer. "*I'd* know better."

Mitch looks at the sky—as much to avoid eye contact as to affect a tragic intensity. "My buddy Spence was getting married, and we took him out for his bachelor party in Niagara Falls and dared him to get one. He said he wouldn't do it unless we all did. So we all did." He takes a swig of his cooler and returns to petting the dog. "Things were different then," he adds, vindicated.

"My god," says the Commodore. "You could get rid of that, you know."

"Well …" he says with the same heroism, "I did some things I regret when I was young. There's sort of a list of reasons I keep it. To remind me to do better."

I'm mid-swallow when he says this, and a chemical high shoots to my brain at the idea that I might be one of those reasons.

"But also," he continues, "Spence died."

No one speaks until the Commodore jiggles the ice in his drink. Mitch takes a breath, self-aware, and addresses the dog. "We were at a rugby party. Like a reunion. Those guys can really drink, I mean …" He clears his throat. "And

Spence, uh, brought two cases of this pink berry wine, 'cause he thought it was funny. You know, he was a big guy."

"Why's that funny?" I ask.

"'Cause it was pink."

"Mm."

"Anyway, he keeps going to the fridge, getting two bottles and chugging them both at the same time. Next thing we're outside and he's naked, 'cause his clothes are so sticky from that shit, and he takes two more bottles, comes out onto the deck, downs them, next thing we know he's on the floor. Like a plank. We thought he was just passed out." Mitch stops and rubs the toe of one sneaker over the other. "But then he starts to pant like he can't breathe and … uh …"

"Jeez," says the Commodore.

Mitch downs the rest of his cooler and Grace compassionately hands him another one, which he cracks open and takes a big slug of, like he's been brave.

"Whaddya gonna do? He shouldn't'a drank so much. Anyway, it was Spence that got me into The Hip, so I have him to thank for that. He was the one into the lyrics. Like, the poetry. And he taught me to sail."

"I'm an asshole," says Grace.

"No," says Mitch. "I'm the asshole."

"I'm sorry, Dad." She leans forward. "I know you miss him."

He pulls her into the crook of his arm and kisses the top of her head.

Then Grace goes for the smoked oysters. "These things, right?" she says. "People try and put them on cucumber slices with dill, or wrapped in bacon or whatever, but they really only go with cream cheese and Triscuits. Not goat cheese or cheddar, not Ritzes or Bretons. Triscuits. Regular Triscuits. Look at that," she says, holding up the Triscuit she's slathered with cream cheese and topped with a big, greasy oyster. She hands it to Mitch. "That's for you," she says. "I made that for you."

He plucks just the oyster from atop the cracker and pops it in his mouth. "Carbs," he says, and pats her shoulder.

She eats the cracker and rolls her eyes.

Mitch doesn't say much else, perhaps feeling like he's shared quite enough already, and just drinks, his mind somewhere else. Grace, by her very presence, rescues the visit.

As the sun sinks on the horizon, the loon from the beginning of "Wheat Kings" calls out from one of the cars, acting as a kind of cue for the members. We wave to them as they file past the Courage toward the clubhouse. An inevitable gloom has set in. The closer we get to the start of the show, the closer we get to the end. The Commodore drains his drink in acknowledgement of the slow, mournful procession.

Mitch has been getting steadily drunker, though he did agree to Grace's suggestion that he drink some water, if only because his diet requires it. I've kept up a watch for Rodney, but he doesn't hang out with the grown-ups. Which means he's just out there. Lurking.

"Guess we'd better make a move," I say. We quietly refill our drinks. Then, as Grace and Mitch go ahead, the Commodore holds me back.

"Here, stay with me a second," he says. I give Grace a wave. He watches them the whole way until they're indoors. We turn to each other, and he motions to the clubhouse with his chin. "I, uh … don't think I can go up there."

"Oh," I say. "Okay."

"I'm not sure I can … watch it."

"Like … the show?"

He nods as if he's surprising himself. "I thought I'd be all right, but I'm not sure now. Here, give me a second." He inhales deeply. The yard is quiet but for the muted din of the CBC pre-show. He exhales and closes his eyes, then opens them. The tendons in his neck tense.

"Nope," he says, the word catching in his throat.

"Try four in, then hold your breath for four, then breathe out for eight."

He tries. "Nope … Can't."

"Take your time."

He's looking at the clubhouse now like a ride he's too scared to get on. "Here, can we sit in yours?" he says, abruptly heading for The Pill.

I open up and we climb down. He settles into the galley and looks into his glass, calmer indoors. I slide in across from him.

"Is it … just too sad?" I ask, in a tone I haven't used with a man for years.

"I'll be blubbing up there in front of everyone."

"We're all sad. If there's a place to be sad right now ..."

He shakes his head.

I reach into the side compartment for the cards.

"Ah," he says as I pull the rubber band from around the deck. "Thank you."

I win the cut. As I deal, he focuses on his hand, assessing the cards he thinks I'll want least so he can throw them in my crib. I peek at his face, imagining what he looks like in the throes of a cry. It's likely monstrous, but the more I try to picture it, the more I wish he'd just give in. Maybe it's just my selfish need to scratch an old itch, but I happen to know it will make him feel better.

It's one of our more subdued games. The Commodore doesn't even seem to relish pegging four of a kind until he sees how far behind I am and the likelihood he'll skunk me. Then he starts in.

"Jeez," he says, dealing what will likely be our last hand before he pegs out. "How's the air back there anyway?" This is one of his standard skunking taunts. He's found his stride. "Little ripe?" Then he remembers. "Speaking of which, I gather Rodney took care of the rabbit situation. See, you just have to give him a little responsibility. You ask him to do something, he'll do it. He's a good kid if he gets the chance."

I drop my head.

"What?" he says.

I give him a long look, grounding myself. "This is not easy to tell you."

"All right."

"Well … it wasn't a rabbit."

"No?" He waits. "Well, what was it?"

I play my jack.

He plays his five.

"Fifteen two," he says hesitantly, and pegs.

"Twenty for two," I say. I peg. "Remember the shark Rodney caught last week?"

He thinks back and nods, holding up his next card.

"I found it," I say, eyes on my hearts, "in his bed."

He slowly lays down his queen, releasing the edge with a *tick*.

"*Rodney's* bed."

"Thirty-one for two. Rodney's bed." I peg the points on my ace, still miles from the finish. The Commodore stares at the melamine for a long time before he lays an eight.

"Eighteen. Last …" I play my ten.

He looks up at me quizzically, then counts without ceremony and pegs out. He doesn't even gloat about the skunking, just stares unfocused at the table. After a minute, he takes off his cap, scratches the back of his head with his pinky, sets the hat on the seat next to him.

"You think he was—"

I cover my ears. We say nothing for a while.

"So where is it?"

"I took it out in one of the Juniors and sank it in a bag with some rocks."

He lifts his long grey brows and cracks a smile. "It's sleeping with the fishes."

"So to speak."

He wipes a hand down his face. "I need to address this, you think?"

"I ... I don't even ..." I hold up my hands. "It's disgusting, but boys are disgusting. Is it more disgusting than the norm? You tell me."

"Maybe he kept it because he's proud of it?"

We're both sad not to believe this.

"Well, I wish you'd have let me know you were going to take it out like the Cosa Nostra." He laughs. "I'd'a liked to have been there." He shuffles the cards and cuts one-handed, a trick he learned from playing with roadies on loading docks. He looks from the deck to me, mid-cut. "You ever have that dream you're carrying around a body in a bag and you don't know where it came from, and you have to get rid of it?"

"What?"

"Yeah, like a gym bag."

I stare.

"I get them all the time," he says, shuffling. "They're pretty common."

"Are you serious?"

"Yeah," he says. "It's, you know, unresolved issues ... fear of change, shame, financial stress—it's not an exact science.

But it's not about the body at all." He tilts his chin and empties his rum. "It's about the burden."

It's as if he's cast a spell—like he's holding up my own thoughts to show me. It's like a drug. I refill our glasses and, with hypnotic ease, say, "Mine go in The Mistake. The bodies."

"Mine go behind the drywall in the clubhouse. It's full of them."

"Wow ..." I say, dazzled. "Wow."

"It's like the forgot-your-skates dream. Isn't that amazing?" he says, holding up his tumbler. "It's not just you!"

I hold up my seagull tumbler to meet his, head swimming, and we toast.

He reaches back and takes his little ponytail out of its rubber band to groom it. "Well, I guess you're going to want a rematch. Losing that bad, I know I would ..."

"Can I cut that thing?" I say, feeling suddenly liberated.

"What, my ponytail?" he asks, palming the uncontained tufts.

"Yeah."

"Off?"

"I have something in mind, and I'm very good. But it *is* your hair."

"Wait, did you cut hair in your shadowy past?"

"I did."

He looks up at me from under his brows in disbelief. "Are you serious? *That's* your secret life? You cut hair?"

I shrug.

"Boy, it's a good thing you waited all this time to drop *that* bombshell," he says, wrapping the rubber band back around his hair. "That's what you did, eh? I thought maybe it was wire fraud. Or cat burglary."

"Huh, you figured me for a thief?"

"Best I could guess. So why not just tell me?"

I take a moment. "One day I will tell you. Today's not that day."

"Intrigue. Even better. All right, Barber of Seville," he says. "Let's see what you got."

"Okay! I'm going to run up first and check stock, though," I say. "Do you want me to put it on the radio? You can turn it off if it's too much." The CBC are broadcasting the show on the radio too, so at least he can keep up. He loves the radio.

"Sure," he says. I tune the portable AM/FM to CBC and turn it toward him next to my bottle of Mount Gay.

I stop on the first step. "This is probably the most private place around here right now, if you happen to think it'll maybe help to just let it out. Have a cry. They're just tears. You're just sad. Let it bend you so you don't break."

"Awful lot of wisdom for one day."

"Yeah, well *babies* have that wisdom. You'll be all alone. I'll knock when I come back."

"Ha ha, Louise." He deals himself a hand of solitaire.

"I'm not kidding."

"Oh. Well, then thank you." He leans his face on his fist and turns a card. "Hair ..."

><

The sky's gone dark, and the sound of crowd noise and newscasters filters through the open clubhouse door past the few members smoking outside. Inside, there's an energy that's half Christmas, half funeral. The whole country right now is either listening to or watching this broadcast. Onscreen, they're showing aerial footage of crowds filling up the parking lot of a rink in Kenora; a kid with a Maple Leaf painted on his face holds a bristol board sign that says IN GORD WE TRUST; a family with three kids are all wearing T-shirts with a crest shaped like a shield, the Maple Leaf in the bottom part and *The Hip* where the name of the highway would go; Toronto Maple Leafs jerseys with BARILKO on the back speckle the crowd. I'm fanning my eyes with my fingers and the show hasn't even started. I hadn't thought to worry about myself, but that's another perk to being on the job; dockmastering during events like this gives me a reason to keep moving in case it gets to be too much.

There's no sign of Rodney in the clubhouse. Mitch and Grace have found themselves a spot by the wall. He's finally taken off his Oakleys, revealing his bleary eyes. They're fixed on his phone, and he's scrolling as a small assemblage of members sits in Grace's tractor beam as she regales them with seafaring tales. Horace Davidson leans in with his mouth open, hanging on her every word.

I dump two more bags of ice in the beer troughs and add another two-four. There are twelve Smirnoff Zeroes tucked in there. Grace waves me over. I hold up a finger, and she gives me an exaggerated wink before bringing her attention back to a breathless Horace Davidson. Program lies beneath the wooden bench.

The crowd in Kingston goes wild, and I look up at the screen where you can see the band backstage, coming down the hall from the green room. Gord Downie is wearing a sparkly silver suit that would make the Commodore slap his knee, and a flat-topped white hat adorned with feathers that, if I know the Great Man, are of Indigenous import. The black-clad tech crew shine flashlights on the band's mic packs, pat their shoulders, and speak into headsets. The crowd is deafening just outside the curtain. Then Gord turns to Rob Baker, the guitar player, takes his face in both hands, and kisses him gently on the lips. I happen to catch Mitch about to take a drink of his cooler when this happens, and he stops halfway to his mouth. Downie pulls Baker into a hug and they hold each other tight, faces pressed into each other's necks. Then Gord Sinclair, the bass player, comes up and Downie takes his face tenderly in his fingertips and kisses him on the lips, then hugs him close. Gord Sinclair squeezes his eyes shut as Downie whispers something in his ear. It's shockingly intimate. I've never seen men show this kind of affection for each other, let alone a rock band. It's like they're waving down to the rest of us from a higher realm, letting us know it's possible. Next, Downie gently cups Johnny Fay's face, and he reaches up and touches Gord's face, and I have to go stock the hand towels.

Passing by their table, I catch another glimpse of Mitch pursing his lips, clearly unsettled by the tender display. A tremor seizes his chin, but he catches himself. He stretches his arms wide, looking for the back of a chair to rest them on, but he's sitting on a bench, so he tucks a hand under each armpit instead.

The crowd gets louder, and the Great Man takes the stage like a knight, his silver suit shimmering in the dark stadium. When the spotlight hits him, the one that will follow him for the rest of the night, he slows down to half speed and turns to face the audience as though they've come upon him unawares. Dawdling contemplatively with a handkerchief, he wryly takes them in, all of Kingston, all of Canada, his gaze direct and curious. He's considering us. Really looking. Then he smiles a slow, wicked smirk, strokes his chin. The band launches into "Fifty Mission Cap," and I can't stop watching now. During the first chorus, I notice the teleprompters all over the stage so he can read the lyrics, because he doesn't know them anymore. No one was sure what to expect tonight. You can tell by the faces in the Kingston audience how important it is that they see he's okay, and he lets them know in his rubbery, strutting way that he's still got it, that he can connect to them without breaking. Giving what they're needing. Every last word, every last note.

To think I was once afraid of this band.

Dean Pearce catches my eye and mouths "Where's Bruce?" with a lift of his shoulders. I look at the ceiling and shake my head like he's off doing something ridiculous. Which reminds me of his ponytail.

As I force myself to move on toward the heads (washrooms), Mitch gets up and walks to the beer trough. He sets his empty bottle on the floor in front of it and opens two more coolers, twisting and pitching the caps without looking. I'll be picking those up later. He turns back to the screen and watches, hauling on one of his drinks, standing with his hips thrust slightly forward, nodding.

For better or worse, he did share that hideous tattoo. And I certainly wasn't expecting the grim details of Spence's final moments. I suppose it takes guts—or at least enough vodka coolers—to reveal that much to relative strangers. Is there a chance he's actually hanging on to that tattoo for the reason he says: to atone?

The band launching into "Courage" catches Mitch off guard, and his face suddenly crumples like it did in my salon chair. It's a big song, and he was probably expecting it to come later. He starts nodding with the angry vigour of a young male fan, as though that's what he's feeling. He's sort of dancing, though it's more of a convulsion, his mouth contorting with rock-and-roll intensity to hide the pain. He chugs the last of his cooler and sets the empty on the ground at his feet. It occurs to me how much tidying his wife must have had to do.

He starts drinking the next one and, I'm not kidding, kicks the other bottle across the floor. As he passes the trough on his way back to Grace and the bench, he grabs another bottle. She looks up at him excitedly—this is his song—and he slaps his thigh twice for the dog, ignoring her, holding the opened and unopened bottles in the same hand. Program slinks out from under the table and jangles happily over to him. I move to the centre of the room and squint out the door to see the dog leaping at Mitch's side as he shuffles toward the spar shed. He trips on one of the low piles of gravel in the yard and does a quick turn to see if anyone saw. I edge to the door, watching with delight as he stumbles away.

Grace waves frantically at me as "Wheat Kings" starts. I point a thumb outside.

The Commodore's hair shouldn't take more than fifteen minutes. There's no denying a part of me looks forward to showing him that I'm good at it. Maybe I'll get myself a new straight razor. I won't open up shop or anything, but something in me wants to be in charge of his hair. Of course I'd never get away without cutting Rodney's hair, with his nightmare double crown, but the idea of touching him right now is beyond me.

Just as I think his name, there's Rodney, sitting next to Dr. Harmon's thirteen-year-old daughter, Cara. They're looking at something on Rodney's phone. I brace my hand on the door frame. Cara's parents are standing up, singing at each other, creating a sort of bower over the two kids, so at least they're supervised. I'm torn watching them, their down-turned faces lit by Rodney's screen. It might have been sweet if I hadn't seen his face up there in the loft earlier today. I'd like to shoot him a threatening look, but I've already stayed too long.

Approaching the boat, I do some extra stomping to announce myself in case by some miracle the Commodore has allowed himself to cry. When I get there, the boards are out, the lights are on, and he's not in there. I hope he doesn't think I abandoned him. The Tall Green One is gone, and the cards are laid out halfway through a hand of solitaire. He must have just needed the break and he's all ready to mingle now. I check the yard and the diesel dock, where he's been known to brood, but he's nowhere to be seen. As I'm scanning, an enormous birch stick comes whizzing end-on-end from behind the spar shed, followed by Program. He rapturously jostles the branch in his mouth, jockeying to keep it level, and then he notices me. And stops.

I want to say that it's the magic of this moment with Program and the look of canine intensity he transmits that entice me over there, but of course it's that Mitch is drunk and alone, and I've stalked this opportunity all night. I cast a final look around, then follow the dog.

Mitch's Nikes are visible from around the corner as Program returns the stick. "Gooboy," he says, followed by a loud snuffle. "Gooboy." Sitting on the ledge of the open bay, he wipes his nose on his arm and reaches for the dog, not quite making contact. Program comes closer. "No, bud," he says petting air and dog. "Not them. You don't kiss your friends. Not your friends."

I pull myself close to the wall.

"S'what girls are for. Girls ... They're dirty ... They'll let you stick it anywhere ... " There's a long pause while the dog pants, then barks, gives a little whine and licks his chops. He's seen this before. When I think how damaged Mitch must be to have these as his intimate thoughts, I almost feel sorry for him. But I'm also reassured that he's truly this rotten inside.

His head bobs again and I move in.

"Hey," I say in my friendly voice.

"Hey." He squints back, then recognizes me. "Yeah, right on. Hey."

I pick up the stick from where Program is dancing and chuck it down the yard. "Guys just having a chat?"

"Uh ... yeah," he says.

"Fun. What were you talking about?"

He has to think back, then chuckles. "Naw ... naw, not girls like you. You're not like that."

"Oh, so you do remember me?"

He nods impishly, like he's cute. Like he's playing a little game.

"From high school."

"Yup."

"Hunh. Okay, that's good. Do you remember apologizing for what you did to me in high school?"

182 · MICHELLE WINTERS

"Um." He giggles. "Yes."

"So, out here, outside the walls of that salon, are you still sorry?"

He labours over this a moment.

"I said it, didn't I?"

"Yes, but does it count? Do you still regret it? Do you still want to do better?"

He points an index finger, peers down it at me. "Too late. You already forgave me."

"Yes, but do you still?"

He takes a drink, annoyed that I'm not playing along. "Jesus …"

A flare of fuel rushes into the chamber. "You know what, I'm not sure I feel so comforted by that apology anymore. Or so forgiving."

"I see."

"Do you remember admitting what a horrible thing you did? And that it's men like you—yourself—that Grace needs protection from? Do you remember saying that?"

He says nothing.

"Does *she* know that?"

A flicker of malice crosses his face. "Does your *boss* know what kind of *work* you used to do?"

"I beg your pardon?"

He lifts his hands smugly. "Hey, *I* didn't say it, it was on the news."

Program drops the stick and I whip it away.

"My god, of all people, you *know* that's not what it was! You were a regular!"

He shrugs. "Just sayin', maybe I didn't know everything that went on there."

The pulse pounds in my temples.

"You know what? I think I'd like to hear that apology again. It really was good."

"You don't get to just keep making me feel bad," he says petulantly.

"No, say what you said." I step closer to him.

He raises his voice. "Jesus, if it's not one of you on me it's another. I just got rid of one nag, and my own kid is at me now. It's just *bick bick bick* all the fucking time." He drinks and points at me. "You know back then, in high school, before we got so *sensitive*, that was just regular teenagers. Girls and boys. Messing around. No harm done."

"No harm done to *you*."

"It wasn't fuckin' ... rape or whatever you wanna call it. And you were pretty into it if I remember ..."

"You know," I say with a steely calm I borrowed from Rodney, "the whole time we were sitting there having drinks, I kept fantasizing about ramming the heel of my hand into your nose, like this." I demonstrate with my hand and nose. "You know what happens when you do that? The bone shards shoot right up into your brain. The cartilage collapses and you go all piggy, all pushed in. And, oh man, does it ever bleed. It'd be just pouring down your chin ... Those membranes are so delicate."

"You're a fuckin psychopath—"

"Say what you said in my chair." I take another step closer. I almost don't care about the apology, I'm just so excited to be this mad.

"No."

"Okay." I pick up the stick from where Program has just dropped it. "But I can't be responsible for what you might do to yourself back here, drunk as you are."

"You wanna fight me, tough guy?" he says, mobilizing. "I don't usually hit girls ..."

I explode in a spluttering laugh, levelling the stick at his chest and jabbing him in the sternum. "Oh, is *that* where you draw the line?" He reaches for the stick and misses. I jab him again. "'Cause I wasn't sure!" He grabs the end of the stick and pulls it, jerking me toward him. As our bodies nearly touch, with all the sustained tension in my muscles, combined with the rush of us being this close, I crouch so our faces are level, pull off, and head-butt him. He reels back, cracking his head against the edge of the open steel door, and slides to the ground like liquid.

My nerve endings swarm to my forehead, pulsing with luxurious pain.

Program runs over and licks Mitch's face, turns twice in a circle, and comes back to me. We face each other, panting. Twinkling stars cloud my eyes. In the magical version with me and the dog, this is where Program tells me there are no witnesses. The coast is clear. Please throw the stick.

Mitch lies there like a doll on the bare-patched gravel, his limbs splayed where his joints allow. I got him right between the eyes, so he's not doing any bleeding. He's just out. His flaccid face tilts toward one shoulder.

"Hey," I whisper. Then louder, "Hey." Nothing. I tap his head with my toe, *boop*, right in the temple. I kick him again. He's actually snoring. I step over to the other side. Program whines, high-pawing around the stick. "Sure, bud," I say. "Just a sec." The cool air fills my nostrils and steam emanates as I fixate on his slackened lips, reflecting on the foulness they've expelled, the sneering they've done—who even knows what else. I bring my foot down gently, then harder, twisting it clockwise, counter-clockwise. His head wobbles along as I grind my sole deeper. I give a good firm push before lifting my foot to see the honeycomb tread on his skin. He breathes regularly and looks weirdly happy. I lift my sneaker higher.

"Louise?"

I bring my foot gently to the ground and Grace takes a step up, backlit by the clubhouse's beacon. Like Cindy Lou Who, she looks at her father, then imploringly at me.

"He's loaded," I stammer.

"Did you just … have your foot on his face?"

For a moment I almost hope for her approval, having witnessed her sanguinary tendencies in action earlier with Rodney. Except that this is her dad. And she loves him.

She's still staring, so I wrestle it out.

"Your father, uh, did something to me when we were in

high school, and—and it was awful, and I … I guess I've never been okay. Since then. I hate to say. I was just going to … I don't know what I was going to do, to tell you the truth. But I know it wouldn't have changed anything."

Her brow knits, and she lowers her forehead, braced for the worst. "What did he do?"

"I don't even think I can—"

"*What did he do?*"

For a second, I consider lying, but she's very hard to lie to. "Seriously, I need to know."

I take a big breath and try to disassociate, simply stating facts.

"We used to wait at the same stop for the school bus, just the three of us, your dad, me and Spence. And the two of them would, every day, say disgusting things about my tits—I mean they said plenty more disgusting things, but I was their main target. And one day, your dad, uh, lured, asked, me out to the woods behind the school, um, and uh, Spence was hiding—and your dad uh, lifted my top and—I'd use the word 'grope' but that doesn't really cover it."

"Ohhhhhh no …" says Grace, covering her mouth.

"To entertain his friend."

She takes a moment to absorb this, her face morphing with disgust. "You've had to spend the whole day being nice to him." Louder, "You had to have drinks with him!" She opens his unopened cooler and hands it to me. "You showed some real restraint with your foot there."

"Thank you." I take a big drink and hand it to her. "I have to tell you, I headbutted him a little. Just a bit. He's fine, look. He's snoring." We contemplate him on the ground. She drinks. "I'll be honest, Grace, I've thought for a long time about beating up your dad. I've thought of doing unspeakable things to him. I'm not proud. And I know it's forever ago, and I'm a grown-up, but all I have to do is picture him, and that urge rises up. I don't think I'll ever shake it."

She nods, someone clearly on her mind. "Yeah ..."

"I saw you put Rodney in a headlock there earlier."

She hands the cooler back. "He pushed me. I reacted—probably too fast. I just, the feeling of some guy putting his hands on me—"

"... I know!"

"—no matter how he might have been kidding around. But I try not to be violent. I don't want to be violent—"

"Oh, me neither."

"No."

"It's ugly—I mean, not when *you* do it—that's like ballet. I don't *need* the violence; but the anger ..." I pinch the air with my bunched fingertips.

"Oh," she touches her collarbone, "I don't know what I'd do without mine."

I take a drink, awash in the buzz of mutuality.

"Well," I say at last, handing back our cooler, "now you know something shitty about your dad, and I'll bet you wish you didn't, and I'm sorry for that."

She takes a deep breath. "Dad's a ... Even if my mom wasn't telling me every day now just what kind of person he is, I'd have figured it out. He's ... got beliefs, you know, from another time. And in case you hadn't gathered, we used to be pretty close. He used to love having me as his little sidekick, teaching me things—boy things. He was the one who signed me up for jiu-jitsu when I was ten. 'There's a lot of bad men out there,' was what he said. But I guess he knew firsthand. I'm glad I learned it, but it sucks knowing *he's* one of the bad ones." She looks at the bottle's label. "These taste like nothing. That's how he gets so drunk. He doesn't realize there's even anything in there." She takes another swig and hands it to me. "I think since I've, you know, *grown up*, his feelings have sort of ... changed toward me. Like we can't be close anymore." She looks at me seriously. "I think he's sexually disgusted by me."

I shake my head. "You are unbelievably perceptive."

"Also, I think he lumps me in with my mom now, which means he thinks I'm against him. We're all against him. And if he doesn't have me, and he doesn't have Mom, he has no one. He doesn't really have friends. People don't take to him 'cause he's so guarded. He doesn't trust, you know? He thinks he *has* something that everyone's trying to take, so he can't get close. It's one of the reasons he gets along so well with animals."

"I'm sorry," I say, unsure who for.

"Yeah, he's pretty insecure. I don't know why—he's got

absolutely everything." She looks to the sky. "Oh, amazing," she says at the first chords of "My Music at Work." She takes another drink, hands me the cooler.

"What's too bad is how much he'd love to be liked. He wishes he could be like Bruce, your Commodore: funny and nice and easy with people. But deep down he believes everyone is just as bad as he is, so he can't open up. He's also terrified of rejection. I'll be honest, I might overdo it a little sometimes just to show we're different," she says. "Don't tell him I said that."

"Don't tell him I stepped on his face."

"Ha, we're good," she says. She goes around the side of her dad and taps his shoulder with her shoe. He mumbles happily. She rolls her eyes.

"I'm scared for him out there, you know? The world is changing and ..." She shakes her head. "He doesn't *know* anything. He's never had to try. He's single now. He's dating online, and oh god, his profile ... I don't know if you've noticed but he's not exactly going gracefully. The tanning and the working out ... god, you should have seen how cute he was when he was younger—"

"I did."

"Omigod that's right. That's so weird."

"It really is."

"He never used to be so buff."

"I know!"

"He works out in the cockpit. He brought a whole set of

free weights. On a boat. For a trip down the coast. He has a thing about being *skinny*. He punishes himself with that word when he hasn't been to the gym, when he's not quite as jacked. Nothing torments him like *skinny*. And we have to make a special trip in every port to pick up more of these coolers for his diet, and he puts that crunchy shit in his hair every morning, even though no one sees him but me—and the thing about travelling in salt water is that no matter how you try to protect yourself, it gets in your hair anyway and makes it crunchy. It's not like he even needs it."

My heart brims. I pass her the bottle.

"When we get to Cape Breton, he's meeting up with a lady he met online and she's going to sail back with him. Trial by fire if there's ever been one, but he needs crew to get home, and Cheryl is into boats. And dogs. I'm a little worried for her, too. Him and my mom were together for twenty years. Other than all the professionals he's been to, he's never dated anyone else. He doesn't know how to be friends with a woman. He doesn't even know it's possible." She drinks.

"Professionals?"

"Oh, tons. He wasn't smart about it either. Mom found that stuff on his credit card statements."

"Well, well, well ..."

"Yeah," she continues fiercely. "*That's* what makes him such a hypocrite for giving me a hard time about my summer job."

"What's your summer job?"

"Webcam."

I stare.

"I'm a webcam girl."

"Oh! Okay."

"I'm not naked or anything!"

"..."

"I have a special skill," she says. "Wanna see?"

She takes another drink and walks up to the path, giggling, then hops up and down lightly from one foot to the other. She looks back over her shoulder. "Okay, watch." With her back to me and her unconscious father, she pulls down the front of her bikini bottoms with her thumbs, and, like a boy, shoots a perfect, steaming yellow arc of pee clean into the air to alight with a crackling in the gravel.

><

Years ago, I was awoken one night to the sound of a long foghorn blast, followed by a few short and another long.

"Lou! LOUISE!" the Commodore bellowed from outside. I threw on my hoodie and stuck my head out the hatch.

"Holy shit!" I said.

"Get out here!" He waved from the rescue Whaler pulled up to my bow. I threw on pants and shoes and scrambled on. He gunned the engine and we tore out into the harbour, his laughter drowning the outboard.

I couldn't believe what I was seeing. The sky above the

horizon was tender green like a baby frog, spreading upward into a luminous yellow, then a vibrant, bloody plum extending to the heavens. The Northern Lights. On the Bay of Fundy. I'd never seen them anywhere, let alone on a river, where the whole spectacle is reflected. "We need to get away from the street lights," he shouted, taking us into The Mistake. "You need to see them where there's no civilization." My eyes laboured to absorb all the magic at once.

As if the sky weren't enough, when the Whaler's bow spliced the waves, they sparkled where we'd cut them like they were bleeding stars. I pointed urgently. "Is that part of it?"

"That's phosphorescence," he yelled. "It's fish!"

"Shit!"

Inside the deepest reach of the cove, he cut the engine. "Ho-lee jeez," he said, neck craned back. "That is some pretty." We sat in The Mistake and laughed. By the time we rode back, we both had dried tears in the hair at our temples from looking up.

Until Grace, I'd never known that wonder could be matched.

✁

"I won't even charge you for that!" she says, shaking her hips like a puppy and pulling up her bikini bottoms, laughing her contagious laugh until we're both making only glottal noises.

"I'd pay good money for that!"

"HA, I love you."

"I love you too, Grace."

I notice her pee trickling down the grade toward Mitch's head. "Oh," I say, "we should probably …" I step giddily down into the ditch and tuck my hands under his armpits, ready to move him, still laughing.

"Oh," says Grace, quickly moving around beside him and dragging her toe through the gravel past his head to create a tributary and divert the stream. "Dad! Ungh, Dad," she says, shaking her own pee off her shoe.

Program, whom I've forgotten about completely, starts up a hearty yap from the water's edge. He's barking at something in the water. It's wearing plaid.

My brain doesn't even send the signal before I'm ripping down the incline to the end of the dock where the Commodore is floating. I throw myself into the air, arms outthrust. Grace runs yelling up to the clubhouse. I get heavy in the water instantly with all the stuff in my pockets, but I have to work with it now. "Hey, hey," I gasp, swimming toward him. I kick the sneaker off each foot to lighten up and then kick and kick and kick. "Guy," I say. "Oh, Guy." His eyes are closed. He doesn't hear me. As I splash toward him, people come hurrying out of the clubhouse to stand at the water's edge. I grab him under an arm and pull him against me, side-stroking endlessly to the launch ramp, where Dr. Harmon is already waiting with the defibrillator. She holds two fingers against his neck. "No pulse," she says, and tears his shirt open. She starts doing compressions, pushing her doubled palms on his chest. Mr. Harmon readies the defibrillator pads and holds them up for her. She brings an ear to his chest and listens. "Still nothing," she says, sticking on the pads and waving for us to stand back.

"Clear," she calls. The shock is delivered. I hold my breath. Nothing. The pack delivers the order to try again. She tries again. "Okay, we've got something," she says as the sirens whine their way down the road.

In the ambulance, I sit sock-footed up front next to the driver, a ragged orange utility blanket around my shoulders. Every few seconds, I check back through the passageway. The Commodore is unconscious but breathing. Tubes snake out of his mouth and a mask covers the whole mess. He hates hospitals and health care in general and would haul all this stuff off his face and chest if he could, for fear it looked like he needed it. I ask the paramedic if she can turn on the radio, and she says they can't because regulations, then picks up an earbud from her coat.

"They're on 'Fiddler's Green,'" she says. I cover my face. This is the Commodore's song.

"Thank you," I say from under my hands.

"I love this one too," she says.

✄

Heart attacks get quick attention, at least. The Commodore is rushed in, and I sit in the waiting room, stuck to the vinyl chair, watching the show on the TV mounted in the top corner of the room. A nurse brings me a set of paper slippers. There's a diverse cross-section filling the other chairs, most notably a family of about twelve, three of them seated, the rest of them standing, pacing, huddled around the triage desk, returning from the cafeteria with trays of Styrofoam cups, always too many cups for the number who need them. Every so often, another person walks through the sliding front doors, looks around frantically, then identifies a family member who, with hands on the newcomer's forearms, delivers an update.

There's a kid who's maybe ten, not part of the big family. He's playing a game on his phone, slumped down into himself so his chins collapse into his neck. He eats a big frosted brownie from the vending machine straight out of the cellophane wrapper with one hand so the other hand can keep playing. In the far corner, a woman my age is sound asleep in a lounger, slumped over like she was dropped there, boneless. Her purse is tucked between her right hip and the chair. I wonder if she's the sick one. I'm drifting a little when I see the kid with the brownie get up and walk over to the woman, his chocolate-covered lower lip protruding. He pokes the woman in the shoulder. He pokes her harder and she snaps awake, sitting up to look past him down the hall. He grasps the sleeve of her sweatshirt, holds it for a second until the woman nods her consent, then he bends down and uses it to wipe the cake off his nose and mouth. She smiles dreamily and ruffles his hair. The kid returns to his seat and resumes his game. She adjusts her purse and goes back to sleep. I close my eyes too, and as I'm fading, the memory of my tenth birthday floats up.

My mother took me out—just us girls—because we hadn't done anything alone together since I'd decided we were on different teams. She wanted to surprise me, so she didn't tell me where we were going. When we got there and I saw the animal paddleboats lined up on the dock, I moaned that I was too old for them but agreed to take out the swan, since we'd come all that way. You're supposed to be accompanied by an adult, but when my mother tried to climb aboard, I put out my hand to stop her. Since I wouldn't relent, and it was my birthday, and because the filthy pond water only came to the thighs of the teenagers working there, they let me go on my own. The attendant gave my mom a shrug.

Technically, one person can paddle the whole boat, but it's not much fun and you don't get anywhere. Nonetheless, I laboured forth a few metres and stopped just outside my mother's reach. She paced along the rope-lined enclosure with the camera, holding it up occasionally, and I'd turn and pedal away. The one photo she managed to get of my face, she laughed as though she'd caught me having fun against my will.

When it was time to come in, my paddle got stuck and one of the teenagers yelled for me to hang on and they'd tow me in. Instead of waiting, I jumped into the filthy water up to my armpits to assert my independence and waded to the dock. When I climbed out, I had a dirt line from the pond's surface on my T-shirt and no towel. I sat wrapped in my mom's London Fog and scowled for the whole drive home.

And she *still* framed the picture.

><

The show is over when I check in at the triage desk. They tell me he's in the ICU and I can go see him, but he's unresponsive. Another nurse takes me to the big room where three other patients are curtained off. He pulls back the cotton drape that reveals the Commodore. Even though I saw him in the ambulance, the sudden picture of his helplessness is a shock.

The nurse motions me off to the side. "We won't know how much function he's lost until he wakes up. But you need to know ... he was out for *a while*, okay?" He tilts his head for emphasis. "The supply of oxygen to his brain was cut off for long enough that there may be ... well, you'll need to manage your expectations. He's sedated, but you can talk to him if you want. Try and keep it positive. There's a chance he can hear you."

I pull the curtain around behind me. His chest rises and falls and the machine beeps vigilantly. I rest my hip against the bed rail. "Hey," I say softly. "Can you hear me? I'll bet you can. I'll bet you're just fucking around in there, aren't you?

Taking a vacation." The squiggle on the heart monitor maintains its rhythmic path: up, down, down, up, down, down. I reach for the hand without the clip pulse thing and pull it heavily toward me. The pads of his palm are callused yellow, warm and dry. His neck is dotted with little moles and skin tags I've never had the impudence to study. The mask over his mouth steams up and empties. I try to picture feeding him.

"You're not staying here, you know," I say, squeezing his hand, "as precious as you think you are. You're going to put on pants and walk out. You're going take your child to the mall and buy him some school clothes. Oh, you're going to hate it." I pull in the little metal chair next to the bed. From somewhere down the hall, "Locked in the Trunk of a Car" plays. The show is long since over, so it could just be a regular broadcast, or someone's phone. "Ha, listen." I point to the air to help him hear. "You think the Great Man dreams about the bodies in the bags too?"

I rest my other hand on his and move in close. "Hey," I whisper. "If you come out of this, I'll tell you the whole thing—the black eye, the whole deal. It's a good story. You'll love it. It's absolutely scandalous."

Something shuffles at the foot of the bed. I pull in closer and watch his toes.

"Can I tell you something, though?" I say, monitoring for movement. "Okay, don't tell anybody this, but Rodney scares the shit out of me." He doesn't register, but I know he's heard. "But also," I pull in closer and tell him extra-confidentially, "you're all I have. I am absolutely fucked here without you."

The curtain rustles and Mr. Harmon appears. I jump back in my chair and think of releasing the Commodore's hand, but can't.

"Hi," he whispers.

"Hey," I say as Rodney appears from behind him and approaches his father's bed, his face inscrutable. Everything happened so fast at the club that I didn't even see Rodney, but I wasn't expecting him to even want to be here.

Mr. Harmon seems to sense this and lifts his shoulders. "He insisted," he says. "After he helped clean up, he asked if we could bring him. He couldn't get a hold of you."

My waterlogged phone sits heavily against my thigh in its cargo pocket.

"He helped clean up?"

He lifts his shoulders again.

Rodney reaches out and touches the strip of tape holding the needle tube on the inside of his father's elbow. I ready a hand.

"He's stable," I say protectively, as though Rodney's presence might threaten his well-being. "He's sedated."

Mr. Harmon says something about tickers and men the Commodore's age as I try to get a read on Rodney, who reveals nothing.

Mr. Harmon waits a moment before he says, "Well ... the girls are waiting out in the car ... Are you two okay?"

"Yeah." I quickly check Rodney. "Thank you."

"Hang in there, big guy," Mr. Harmon says to the Commodore. Then he puts a hand on Rodney's shoulder, as though bestowing a long-anticipated right. "Looks like this makes you the man now." You'd think he'd know better than to make a stupid comment like that in a moment like this, especially with his wife being the doctor. Rodney gives him an uncertain smile.

Once the curtain closes, Rodney's mouth twitches, quivering briefly before dissolving into a squiggly ribbon. His shoulders quake, and he tilts forward like a reed. "Lll …" he keens. "Llou, I was …" —he covers his eyes with his forearm and his lips undulate out of control—"… so shitty to him …"

"Oh, bud …" I stare openly at Rodney's fearless display. "Can he hear me?"

"… I think so."

"Dad." His face contorts, his voice an airy squeak. "I'm so sorry …" He reaches for the Commodore, but the wires and needles are in the way, so he holds out his limp arms, spasming with his sobs, before finally wrapping them around himself, which is more than I can bear.

"Here," I say, still stupefied by the readiness of both his tears and his apology. "Come here."

The bed is between us, so he has to come around it. He extends his arms to their full length, and I walk into them with mine outstretched. It's unnatural at first. I try to keep my breasts from getting involved, but something melts the space between us, and I soften and move in. He lays his head on my shoulder and cries harder; he feels less alien. "It's okay," I say, reaching up to stroke the feathery curls his dad would once have had. I'd give the ends a point cut, sliding upward to soften the shape and take out some of the weight. I'd leave some length in his double crowns, letting the hair fall the way it has no choice but to do, and trim into it to blend it with the rest. My soul lightens.

"Do I have to go ... live with Mom and Geoff?" He sniffles as his sobbing subsides.

"Of course not. You don't have to go anywhere. Your dad's coming *home*," I say, the word sounding oddly new. "But look, it's going to be you and me around there for a while. We need to get along."

"We get along."

"We need to treat each other with the same respect."

"Okay."

"Will you help out around the club without giving me grief?"

"Can I get paid?"

Hadn't even occurred to me. "Of course. Oh, of course."

We settle back into the hug and enter a new phase where we're just leaning on each other. Of course. He's searching for limits. He wants a job, and privacy, like any normal kid. I imagine going to visit him in a university dorm decorated with Kubrick posters, attending his wedding, talking with him about politics.

"I guess we're sort of family now," he says.

I hold him tighter. "Yeah, I guess."

"So," the realization slowly dawns on him, "I guess this does make me the man now."

I bring my mouth to his ear and tighten my grip on his occipital bone. "No, bud," I murmur. "That's me."

ACKNOWLEDGEMENTS

Enormous thanks to:

bell hooks, for "The Will to Change," whose thesis helped define Constance and the very idea of *Hair for Men*.

The Canada Council for the Arts and the Ontario Arts Council for their generous support.

Mary "T" Brodkorb, Kevin Cogliano, Judy Cook, Lori Delorme, Al and Anne Drew, Ann and Wayne Fulton, Jillian Hall, Sara Levine, Lucy Luck, Andrew David MacDonald, Alexander MacLeod, Laura Martin, Jennifer Nason, Alison Pick, Michael Redhill, Emma Rose at the Cabinet Salon, Shirarose Wilensky and everyone at House of Anansi Press— all you beauties for your wonderful reasons.

Leigh Nash for finding the books in my writing and making them happen at all.

Chris Harms for making the sun come out.

The Hip for the songs.

© Chris Harms

MICHELLE WINTERS is a writer, painter, and translator born and raised in Saint John, NB. Her debut novel, *I Am a Truck*, was shortlisted for the 2017 Scotiabank Giller Prize. She is the translator of *Daniil and Vanya* and *Kiss the Undertow* by Marie-Hélène Larochelle. She lives in Toronto.